TROUBLE
TOMORROW

D0774556

TERRY WHITEBEACH & SARAFINO ENADIO

TROUBLE TOMORROW

ALLEN&UNWIN
SYDNEY · MELBOURNE · AUCKLAND · LONDON

First published by Allen & Unwin in 2017

Allen & Unwin
83 Alexander Street
Crows Nest NSW 2065
Australia
Phone: (61 2) 8425 0100
Email: info@allenandunwin.com
Web: www.allenandunwin.com

A Cataloguing-in-Publication entry is available from the
National Library of Australia
www.trove.nla.gov.au

ISBN 978 1 7602 9146 4

Teachers' notes available from www.allenandunwin.com

Cover and text design by Debra Billson
Cover photos: portrait of boy © Baymler/Getty Images, tank © John Wollwerth/Shutterstock, barbed wire © ewastudio/123RF, road © Triff/Shutterstock
Internal photos: tank and village © John Wollwerth/Shutterstock, sunrise © Peter Schwarz/Shutterstock, barbed wire © ewastudio/123RF
Map by Guy Holt
Set in 11.5/14.5 pt Adobe Garamond by Midland Typesetters, Australia
Printed in Australia by McPherson's Printing Group

10 9 8 7 6 5 4 3 2 1

The paper in this book is FSC® certified.
FSC® promotes environmentally responsible,
socially beneficial and economically viable
management of the world's forests.

Trouble Tomorrow was redrafted as part of a Creative Time Residential Fellowship provided by the May Gibbs Children's Literature Trust.

For all our relations

SUDAN

ETHIOPIA

SOUTH SUDAN

Juba •
• Torit
• Lokichogio
• Kakuma

SOMALIA

UGANDA

KENYA

Dadaab •

• Nairobi

TANZANIA

N

0   400 km

OBULEJO DREAMS *he is with his friend Riti, hauling in spangled tilapia fish, his dusty feet cooled by the tumbling waters of the Kinyeti River. The sun presses on their heads and shoulders, and in the distance the peaks of Imatong stand tall and serene. A little further along the riverbank, groups of boys are dashing in and out of the water, splashing and calling to each other.*

Tat-tat-tat-tat! Brrrmm! Rrrrr! Ul-lu-lu-lu-lah!

Obulejo slams awake, heart racing, and scrambles up off his mat.

Gunshots and screams jab the air. Flashes of light pierce the darkness.

The Rebels!

Other boys in the dormitory are jumping up, calling or whispering urgently in the dark. Snatching up his shirt and sandals, Obulejo ducks between them to reach the door. He dashes across the schoolyard, clearing the perimeter fence in one startled-gazelle leap and landing on the soft red soil of the road by the school compound – where he finds himself swept along in a noisy stampede of townsfolk running for their lives.

Darting lights flash through the laneways and compounds, and the noise is terrific – the crack and boom and din of weapons,

1

cries of panic and fear. Shells whizz through the chilled air, streak red the blackness. Bullets thud into walls. Obulejo stumbles over fallen bodies as he runs, collides with the walls of buildings, is snatched, jostled, pushed and shoved by the mob. Mothers screech their children's names; people yell for family members to come now, right now!

His nostrils burn with the stink of cordite and his feet hardly touch the ground as the terrified crowd surges through the town centre, veering past the barracks and the banners of the town stadium, the Midran Huria, making for the outskirts of town.

He is sobbing for breath, tripping, stumbling, bleeding, but he dare not pause; he must outrun this nightmare that has ripped his quiet sleep to shreds.

Run for the shelter of the hills.
Run for his life.

1

THE FIRST TIME the Rebels come, a messenger brings the news.

'Run! They're on their way!'

It is early evening. Obulejo's mothers and sisters are busily clearing up after the meal, the men drinking sweet tea while the younger boys kick a ball around the compound.

Obulejo's father Moini springs into action. He hustles his two wives and all the children out of the compound and into the banana plantation, beyond the compound fence.

'We will be safe here,' Moini tells them. 'The soldiers will not search the gardens. It is houses and stores they'll be wanting to plunder.'

He signals them to hunker down in the darkness under fallen fronds, out of the bright moonlight. As they wait, they hear the thud of marching boots and the crack of gunfire.

The stamping and shouting get closer.

'Stay low,' Moini whispers. 'Don't make a sound.'

Obulejo puts his arms round his little sister Izia and pulls her close. If only the older brothers Lino and Jaikondo were not so far away in Egypt. But Baba is strong and clever. He won't let the soldiers harm them.

They stay in the plantation all night, crouched in the dark listening to the shouting, the gunfire and the thud and slam of buildings being attacked and granaries broken open.

Obulejo barely registers the harsh prickliness of the palm fronds through the cloth of his shirt, the cloying darkness of the night, the cramp in his calves as he huddles with his family; he is too busy straining to detect how close the soldiers are. As the din of their boots gets louder a sweaty panic engulfs him. If the Rebels discover his hiding place, they will haul him off to war. He's fifteen – old enough to fight. Boys as young as seven have been taken as soldiers.

This time they are lucky. The Rebels are just passing through.

At dawn, Obulejo and his family creep back home. Their huts are undamaged but the granary door is hanging askew and most of the maize and sorghum are gone.

'How is it with you?' Moini calls out to their neighbours. 'Is anybody hurt?'

'No, but my goat is missing!' one calls back.

'Our cooking pots are gone!' says another.

A cry goes up. 'They have taken all our warm blankets.'

'May God forgive them!'

'Ai-eeh!'

But at least nobody has been badly injured or killed.

Moini goes to work as usual that morning, warning his wives to take care and stay alert.

To the children he says, 'You must not be afraid. Did I not protect you when the soldiers came? I am your father and I will take care of you.'

Obulejo wants to believe his father's promise, and during the day, as he recites his lessons, and later helps collect wood for the fire, he can mostly forget the night's fear, but when darkness falls and he settles to sleep with his brothers and sisters, he finds himself jerking awake at the slightest noise.

At the squeak and scamper of rats in the thatch, the plop of frogs in the water barrel or the call of a night bird, he finds himself suddenly awake, wide-eyed, staring into the dark, his mind churning over and over the events of the night before.

The elders sit nearly all night by the fire, talking in low voices. Obulejo strains to catch scraps of their conversation in the rise and fall of the accented Arabic that all the tribesmen hold in common.

'Our ancestors came to me in a dream, to warn me,' one uncle says, 'my father's father and his – just as they did before Anyanya – the Poison War.'

'Ai-ee-ah!' Obulejo's senior mother wails. 'I lost my father then and now I will lose my husband!'

'Hush, my wife,' Moini cautions her. 'Do not wake the children with your woman's wailing. The Rebels are far away by now.'

'But what if they return?' Uncle Eriga asks. 'We must gather the family and flee south before this pestilence swallows our village whole.'

The rumbling voice of an Acholi elder joins in. 'Why run like frightened women and leave our houses and crops for the Lotuko tribesmen here?'

The discussion next turns to weaponry – armoured vehicles, machine guns, assault rifles: MG 3s, AK-47s.

'They say the soldiers are ordered to fire into the air, to avoid civilians,' Uncle Ochola says, 'but always townsfolk and villagers are caught in the crossfire.'

The voices descend to a murmur and Obulejo drifts back to sleep.

Suddenly a rooster starts crowing. Obulejo's eyes snap open. His heart thuds. Unbidden, there comes an image of his little sister Izia lying blood-spattered in the village street.

No matter how hard he tries, he cannot get that picture out of his mind.

Obulejo tries to keep his fears to himself but he can't help noticing that a hut prepared for his favourite uncle has lain empty for months and when Uncle Sylvio still does not arrive and Obulejo asks his father why, Moini brushes the question aside.

Mama Natalina tells him not to speak of it to anyone.

Soon after, there is wailing somewhere in the village. Then Obulejo overhears something that fills him with dread.

'Tortured,' he hears one man whisper to another. 'Then bound and gagged and carried high up over the desert in an army plane and pushed out to his death.'

The other man waggles his head in grim affirmation. 'And no one knows where the body lies.'

Obulejo imagines telling Uncle Sylvio this silly scary story and Uncle laughing and saying, 'It was not me those men were talking about. See. Here I am. You worried for nothing.'

But his uncle does not come. And the next time Obulejo mentions him, Moini says, 'Do not speak of your uncle again.' His face is grim.

Every day after school Obulejo goes with the other boys on the long walk to the family garden plots, to guard the *godo* plants from hungry birds and marauding creatures.

They light fires, flick dried mud-balls through the papery leaves of the sorghum and sing and shout to scare the birds. These boys are his friends but he dare not mention his uncle, even to them.

Then in the *seri* times, when the maize is ripening, the children's job is to chase off the baboons, the *lore*, that come to raid the grain. As a child, Obulejo was afraid of those grimacing creatures and even now he is older he still feels a tremor of fear when he sees their gangling arms, their scowling faces and their sharp pointed teeth that can tear a child apart. Now he fans the flames, shouts and hulloos and waves his stick with his friends, till the baboons, snarling horribly, are forced to slink away into the shelter of the trees.

When he was young, Obulejo's older brothers teased him for his fear of the *lore*. 'Never will you have the courage of a warrior if you fear the *lore* so much!' they laughed. But the rumours he and his schoolfriends now swap with each other as they walk home from the gardens at dusk are more terrifying than a thousand baboons.

Every one of the children has overheard veiled conversations in the market, on the road, in their family compounds, in fireside discussions late at night or before school in the early morning. An old man in Juba dragged away and shot, and his wife killed the next day; a father kidnapped; child soldiers raping girls and women and shooting their own clansmen or being forced to slaughter family members; men tortured with burning tyres around their necks; a man bludgeoned with rifle butts; women and babies chopped with pangas; dead bodies lying bloated on riverbanks.

As a child, Obulejo listened to stories of ghosts and monsters and spirit ancestors, told by the aunties and uncles, but what he is hearing now, he thinks, is real killing, not just made-up stories.

Sometimes his terror turns to rage. 'The Dinkas are the cause of all our troubles,' he says to his friend Riti. 'That Colonel Garang and the Sudan People's Liberation Army, if they had not started up the war again, everything would be all right.'

'No it wouldn't,' Riti retorts. 'Then the Arabs would rule us and we would all be under sharia law, having our hands chopped off and not being allowed to walk about freely.'

'What about the Rebels?' Obulejo shouts. 'The Dinkas are Sudanese but they're killing other Sudanese people. If I had a gun I'd shoot them all, right now!'

'And killing the Dinkas would bring peace?' Riti says.

'Well, are we to just sit and wait and allow ourselves to be killed, then?'

Riti sighs. 'Forget about the Dinkas. It all started long before we were born, and anyway, there's nothing we can do to change things. Come on, let's go fishing.'

2

NOT LONG AFTER *seri* harvest-time, word comes that the Rebels are heading towards the village again.

'Keep the children close,' Moini tells his wives. 'Do not let the little ones stray from your side unless the older children are with them.'

That night, no one leaves the compound. They cluster around the fire, backs to the darkness.

Next day, village life continues much as usual. Fathers work in the timber mill, dig garden beds and mend roof-thatches. Mothers tend the gardens, grind maize, attend to household chores. Obulejo and his schoolfriends continue with their lessons, fetch water and watch over their younger brothers and sisters.

'Even if the soldiers come back,' Moini reassures his family, 'it will just mean a day or two in hiding. Then everything will return to normal.'

He is wrong.

The next time is different.

One morning Moini leaves for work as usual, but not long afterwards he re-enters the compound, shouting for his children and his wives.

'Hurry,' he tells them when they come running. 'Pack food and clothing and blankets. We have no time to lose. The company has organised a bus to take us down to Torit. This village is no longer safe.'

The women gasp and cover their faces. Obulejo's head spins: this morning began as just another ordinary day and now they are about to leave the mountains – perhaps forever. These may not be his people's lands but he has lived in this Lotuko village, far from the Ma'di lands, nearly all his life, since his father took the job at the mill. Is anywhere safe?

Obulejo races back inside the hut and stuffs his notebooks and pencils and maths textbook into his school satchel. He grabs a blanket and a pair of shorts and then runs to help his sisters and mothers. The older sisters, Foni and Anzoa, are not coming with them; they are going to hide in the mountains with Foni's husband's family. Obulejo hears people in nearby compounds shouting and running. Goats bleat and chickens squawk as they scuttle out from under flying feet.

The families quickly assemble outside the mill manager's office and scramble onto the waiting buses. Anzoa and Foni hug their weeping mothers goodbye.

The buses take off, rumbling over the rough road out of the village. Looking out the window, Obulejo sees Lotuko tribesmen beginning to leave. They are going the other way – up into the mountains. This, after all, is their land and has always been so. They will not leave it, Rebels or no Rebels. They will take refuge in caves and mountain strongholds and wait out the danger as they did during the Poison War, before Obulejo was born.

The cavalcade of cars and buses carrying Obulejo's family and others winds through steep mountain passes and round hair-raising bends down to the plains. The road is a mess of ruts and flooded surfaces and on one tight bend Obulejo's bus threatens to topple into the deep ditch. At each stream, as they approach a makeshift bridge, Obulejo's mothers close their eyes and begin to intone, 'Hail Mary Mother of God . . .' until the bus bumps and rattles safely across.

The journey seems endless to Obulejo, but even more so to his little brother Amoli, who begins to fret. Obulejo puts his arm around Amoli and starts a long story about tricky Mr Hare.

'Once upon a time,' Obulejo begins, 'Mr Hare and his son Abunibeebee went hunting in the forest. It started to rain heavily and they did not have a fire to warm themselves. Mr Hare saw a fire burning in a log far away and he said to his son, "Go and fetch it." "All right," Abunibeebee replied, and went to fetch the fire. But it wasn't a fire. It was the red teeth of the Lion!'

Amoli is soon drawn into the story. Obulejo holds him close. With Izia balanced awkwardly on his knee, her sleepy head banging against his shoulder, his other arm soon begins to ache, but he dare not disturb her lest she wake and begin to cry.

At long last they reach the plains and finally trundle onto the main street of the district capital, Torit. People stream out to meet them, calling out questions, anxious to learn the fate of their relatives in the mountain village.

'It is deserted,' Moini tells them. 'Everyone has fled.'

'The Lotuko are hiding in the bush,' Uncle Eriga adds. 'They are at the mercy of the Rebels. May God protect them.'

People begin to discuss fleeing south to Uganda or east to Kenya. Obulejo has heard his father talk of the family's hurried move from their Ma'di lands during the Poison War. And now it seems they have to run away all over again.

Family members are not even all together. His brother Juma is in high school in an area now in the hands of the Rebels, the two older brothers are in Egypt, at Cairo University, and most of the grandparents are in the capital city, Juba, or have crossed the border into Uganda, with other members of their clan. Where can Obulejo, his parents and the younger children go next? If the Rebels catch up with them, his father and uncle will be pressed into service as soldiers; and he will be, as well. Who will look after his mothers and the younger children?

His family already has been torn apart by the war. Now the bonds are fraying further. Will they ever be able to get back together again?

Torit is much bigger and busier than the Lotuko village they have come from. Obulejo has never seen so many buildings crowded together.

The air smells different too – stickier and warmer than the spicy coolness of the mountains. The river washes lazily across the western road, slow and tepid. No rushing torrents here, tumbling over rocks, just languid spillages, easy for washing and bathing. Here and there are pools deep enough for fishing.

Moini finds shelter for the family in a compound with other mill workers, and life in the new town begins to assume a routine. Obulejo likes to explore the bustling markets with his friend Riti, and to watch soccer matches, marches and military parades in the Midran Huria. The marshalling of police and troops each morning in the barracks always draws a small crowd of onlookers too.

One morning Riti comes to say goodbye. 'We are going south,' he says.

Obulejo stares at him in horror. 'We have been friends our whole lives. You can't go.'

But they both know there is nothing they can do, so they clasp each other's hands and promise they'll be together again one day. And then Riti is gone.

Without his best friend, the days seem to stretch on forever.

Obulejo is angry. He tells Amoli, 'The war has stolen my friend.' Amoli looks at him with big round eyes. 'Just like Mr Hare stole everyone's *seri*?' But Obulejo has no patience with stories. When he tells his brother to leave him alone, Mama Josephina scolds him for being unkind to the little ones.

Everyone is edgy. Moini tells Obulejo to stay close to home, it is not safe for him to wander about on his own, and a few days later secures a place for Obulejo in a good school, close to the church and the main market square.

'You will be safe in Torit,' he tells Obulejo. 'The police and soldiers guard the town well, but it is different for me and your uncle. We must move on and look for safety in Juba, or cross the border into Uganda.'

Obulejo's heart contracts with dread. 'Mama Natalina and Mama Josephina and the little ones too?'

Moini nods. 'I cannot stay here and let my family go hungry. I have no local rights or land to grow crops and no real chance of a job here. And it is dangerous for me to remain. There are many who envied my position at the mill and claimed it was unfairly given to a Ma'di "foreigner". Now that I am no longer under the protection of the owners, these people will look for any opportunity to harm me, to get revenge.'

Obulejo's cheeks flush with rage. If people are so jealous why don't they go to school and study like his father and get themselves a good job? And now all this fighting has taken his friend Riti away and it's spoiling his family's life.

Later, when Obulejo brings water to Mama Josephina, he finds her weeping. 'I curse the day we must leave another of the sons behind,' she wails. 'Too many of the family already are far out of reach.'

'Hush, Mama,' he tells her. 'Weeping will not change my father's mind.'

'Your father says all our sons are to be educated men,' Mama Josephina says, 'and truly I respect my husband's wishes, but —'

She spreads her hands out in a gesture of despair. Obulejo goes off to fetch her a second *kere* of water and when he returns with the overflowing gourd she has dried her tears, and is busy again about her chores with Mama Natalina, the senior wife.

Mama Natalina tries to explain Moini's decision. 'The old days, when school was not considered necessary, are gone.'

'But I myself went straight from my father's to my husband's compound before I was full-grown,' Mama Josephina says. 'No school for me.'

'These are new ways,' Mama Natalina reminds her, 'and it must be as our husband says.'

'Please God the priests will keep Obulejo safe, then,' Mama Josephina cries.

Mama Natalina nods. Up to now the Rebels have respected the sanctuary of the church.

Obulejo feels torn. Everybody is disappearing. His best friend Riti, the older brothers and sisters; and now Baba and the rest of the family. If only he could go too. He dreads remaining in Torit on his own. But his father's wishes are law. Boarding school it must be.

Amoli and Izia cling to him, and Obulejo tries to be especially kind to them, that final day. He piggybacks Izia around tirelessly and tells Amoli at least a dozen Mr Hare stories, making his brother laugh at the escapades of wily Ito – Mr Hare – and his wife Emozia.

The mamas pat and hug him. 'We will miss you, our son,' they whisper, as huge fat tears roll down their cheeks.

Next day, Moini bids his son farewell. It is a solemn moment.

'It is very important not to break your education. You must study hard and bring honour to your family, my son.'

'I will,' Obulejo promises.

'The day will come when by God's grace we will be brought back together again.'

'Yes, Baba.'

But even as Obulejo says this he is seized by an unreasoning dread that this is the last time he will ever see his father or his mothers or Amoli or Izia.

3

ST XAVIER'S IS much larger than Obulejo's old village school, but the teachers and students are welcoming. His Acholi friend Ochan has just started at St Xavier's as well, and within days they become firm friends with two Lotuko boys, Lolika and Ohisa, who tell them the teachers' nicknames and show them the choicest fishing spots and the market stalls that have the best bargains.

The new routine begins to absorb Obulejo. Lessons and prayers fill each school day, and there's study and preparation in the evening, till the paraffin in the lamp runs out or his eyes get too heavy to keep reading. Then he folds his shirt, places it beside his sandals and lowers himself onto his sleeping mat. That's when the images crowd in, the memories of the night in the plantation, the panic as the news of the Rebels' approach swept through the village, the hurried escape and bumpy bus ride and the stricken look on his parents' faces when they left him in Torit.

The night air is closer, thicker, down here on the plains, making it harder for Obulejo to sleep. An owl calls, 'Ooh-OOH, ooh-OOH,' and he immediately wakes and stares into the thick darkness. Everything seems wrong: no cricket-chirp, no

rat-scuttle in the thatch, no firefly-glow. Then he remembers –
he is at St Xavier's, and somewhere to the north-west his family
is searching for a safe place to hide. 'Merciful Father, please
protect them,' he prays, and sleeps again.

And wakes to the unbelievable din. Armoured vehicles
roar, machine guns jackhammer, the rapid fire of the Rebels'
Kalashnikovs punctuates the slower and heavier boom of the
army MGs.

Rebel anthems swell; the defending government soldiers
yell defiance.

People scream in terror.

Obulejo does the only thing he can do – he runs for his life.
Out of the dormitory and into the road, where the panicked,
struggling crowd hurtles him past the Midran Huria and out
towards the town boundaries. 'Torit is burning!' someone
yells and the crowd screams even more wildly. Bullets sing
and thwack. People collide and stumble.

Above the din, police are bellowing, 'Come out of your
houses!' 'Leave the house at once!' 'Go! Now!'

Along with everyone else Obulejo rushes out of the
burning town and across the fields of sorghum stubble into
the concealing thickness of the tall savannah grass. People
press forward, close packed and panting, as they fight through
the endless grasslands, nostrils choked with dust, parched
stems smacking against their bodies, and scramble up into the
hills. For over an hour they run without pause from the town,
surging up the final hillside into the rays of the blood-red
rising sun. Only when the highest slope is gained do the
frantic runners at last begin to slacken their pace.

Gasping and panting, Obulejo flops down behind a
sheltering tussock as others crawl under bushes. Mothers draw

their wide-eyed children close. Older folk hobble up last and drop to the ground, wheezing as they try to catch their breath.

Silence descends – silence broken intermittently by brutal bursts of gunfire on the plain. Dense plumes of smoke rise from huts and buildings in the distance.

No one speaks. All are held by the same terror.

Obulejo is struggling to make sense of things. His mind hurtles crazily about, unreeling furiously like the string of a kite as it strains for the freedom of the skies, bobbing and spiralling in agitated curves. His ears still ring from the crack of weaponry, the roar of tanks and trucks, the Rebels' patriotic songs and slogans, the defiant shouts of the government troops. Townspeople screaming, crying, calling for relatives and neighbours. The police bellowing orders: 'Leave your houses!'

Before his eyes, images of the surging crowd still dance: frantic parents clutching bundles, dragging their children, babies slung onto backs, old people hobbling, stumbling, falling behind – left to the mercy of God or the Rebels.

Obulejo's muscles continue to pump as he mentally gallops the miles from the town to the temporary sanctuary of the foothills again and again – swifter than any school sports race he ever ran, faster than he'd need to move to evade a cobra's strike.

Outrunning death.

A maelstrom has torn everything familiar and normal from his grasp, and flung him into a waking nightmare.

Blood thumps through his veins and arteries, his chest heaves, his hands clench and unclench. He is covered in cold sweat.

Smoke from the besieged town spirals upward. Vultures wheel low in the smudgy air. Around him, terrified townsfolk are concealed in the underbrush. Below, the sacked town and the Rebel soldiers: broken and abandoned dwellings, soldiers with guns.

A few hours ago he was part of another existence; a world of lessons, studies, sports, church, bustling markets, tribesfolk who tended their gardens and herds and called to each other from their compounds. A world in which fathers set off to work early each morning and mothers sang as they slapped the clothes clean, or ground *sim-sim* into *fura* – flour – and stirred pans over the fire. A world of bird call and sunshine, orderly and predictable. That world is gone. In its place is a new, alien world of turmoil and panic.

Obulejo buries his face in the damp soil. For several minutes he feels nothing but the rhythm of his own beating blood.

Run! it pulses.

Go! the torn soles of his feet echo.

Now! throb his aching lungs. *Move! Go!*

But he cannot. Impaled on the hillside, breath sobbing in his throat, he crouches, like a small soft animal run to ground by hunters, waiting for the coup de grâce to fall.

CLACK-CLACK! *Clack-clack!*

Obulejo starts, sick with fright at the sudden sound, then almost sobs with relief. It's only the long, dry seedpods of the rattling mimosas overhead.

As he lets out a long breath, he observes with dull surprise that his legs and feet are cut to ribbons. He felt nothing while he was running. Now the lacerations begin to throb.

His throat burns too. It is hours since his headlong flight and the sun is getting higher, but he dare not venture out to search for water. He has no food either. He has only the shorts he is wearing, his school shirt and sandals dangling from one wrist.

He licks his dry lips. What now? If only he could think clearly. One thing he knows; there is no way to get word to his family, to let them know what has happened or where he is. He is on his own. Until now there have been others to guide and steady him – Baba and the mamas and uncles, older brothers, the clan, the tribe. Never has he been just a boy alone.

His mind reels at the idea. A boy without family, without *joti alu kaka*, the one door through which all family members enter and claim the safety of the hut. Alone is unthinkable to a Ma'di boy. Alone is unsafe, like a tethered goat in lions' territory. Alone means death.

Suddenly, he feels a light touch on his wrist. He swings around. It is Auntie Juan, a Kuku woman, a friend of his parents, her eyes peeping through the leaves and her skinny arm extending from the depths of a spreading bush. She is holding out a *kere* of water. Her other arm follows, a small handful of *godo* on her open palm. Obulejo smiles his thanks and takes a sip from the *kere* and a small mouthful of sorghum paste.

The water feels cool on his tongue, loosens his parched throat. The porridge soothes his empty belly. But it is Auntie Juan's kindness that eases his heart.

Obulejo parts the branches of the bush cautiously. Auntie's children are huddled around her. They stare at Obulejo with big eyes. Obulejo smiles at them. Auntie Juan whispers her children's names. The baby, Keji, buries her face in her mother's shoulder. Auntie Juan nods to Obulejo. He nods back. This small woman and her children must be his family for now. Her kindness has made her a mother to him, and he a son to her.

He wriggles close and shows the older children a silent game with fallen leaves, leaving Auntie Juan free to attend to her fretting baby. Keji settles at her mother's breast and for a moment, in their insecure hiding place, a little peace reigns.

Soon they must leave the hillside, Obulejo knows, get further away. But where to?

If only he could wake to the morning prayer bell, and rise and file in to chapel with the rest of his classmates. But the town Obulejo has called home for the last three months is probably a smouldering ruin now.

He cannot stay and take his chances here; he must get further into the hills. But although he aches to be up and away, his limbs will not obey. Is he to die here on this hillside?

The decision is taken out of his hands.

From his hiding place he begins to notice subtle movement along the hillside. Leaves waver tremulously and almost imperceptibly, tall grass stems are being parted by half-hidden hands, and branches are briefly and silently pulled aside. Then comes a series of soft, low sounds: susurrations of grass stalks gently rubbed together, subdued imitations of bird calls, whispered names of mothers, aunties, children, grandchildren.

Should he reveal his position? It might be a trap. More and more signals are passed surreptitiously along, from person to invisible person. Few dare show themselves. Everybody is edgy.

Then, 'Psst,' comes a sibilant whisper, close to Obulejo's ear. It is Auntie Juan. The decision has been made, she tells him. They are to push on further into the mountains and try to find a way through the dense jungle to the east. Make their way to Kenya if they can. Although it will be more than one hundred and fifty miles to walk, it's the only possible escape route.

At the prospect of entering the jungle, Obulejo's bowels contract with dread. There will be animals far more fierce than the *lore* there. But they can't just perch on this hillside waiting for the Rebels to pluck them off like ripe mangoes.

One by one, people start to crawl out of their hiding places, keeping low to the ground. The adults gather in a tight huddle and begin to talk in urgent whispers. Obulejo strains to hear what they are saying. There is not much time.

They dare not remain so close to the besieged town. Patrols may already be on the way.

A tall, long-limbed older man seems to be the main spokesman.

'Do you know him?' Obulejo whispers to Auntie Juan.

'Kuku man,' she whispers back. 'His name is Lege. He knows the Lotuko lands well.'

'How deep are the rivers? Are there rapids?' one woman asks Lege, clutching her two small children.

'Is the bush passable?' asks another.

As Lege answers each question, more are flung at him.

'Can we get through?'

'How will we find food?'

'Must we climb many mountains?'

The sun creeps higher into the sky and Obulejo burns with impatience. Are people going to just sit and yabber all day long, while the Rebels catch up with them?

Still more questions come.

'Surely we are too many to go undetected?'

'Dare we risk breaking cover?'

'Will the soldiers come after us and capture us?'

'How long will the fighting continue?'

Eventually, Lege holds up his hand. 'We must act quickly. Cover is scant here and we may be set upon at any moment. We need to get away into the mountains where the bush is dense and tangled, where no one can track us easily.'

Then how will we be able to make our way? Obulejo thinks. But they must.

Crouched close to Auntie Juan and her children, Obulejo wonders how long they will have to keep walking and what will happen to the children. Will they be strong enough to keep going? Will Auntie be able to find food in the bush or will her children die of hunger? And Obulejo himself, a boy on his own, travelling further and further away from his family – how will he fare?

Have my parents heard what has happened yet? he wonders. *There is no way they will be able to come and look for me. Even if word has reached them. If they are still alive.*

He quickly pushes this last thought away. He cannot afford to think such things. He must not let his mind go beyond this moment. The only thing that matters right now is to get moving.

People start to get to their feet, gather their bundles, hoist babies onto their backs. A few, like Obulejo, have sandals to put on, but many must go barefoot.

Obulejo sees heads bowed in prayer and catches whispers of ancestor invocations. Obulejo remembers his father speaking about the crossed spears and water spilled on the ground, the old rituals the chief followed to invoke good hunting for the tribe. Now what they must hunt for is safety – and what they need to find is a place of protection.

An image of his father's face pierces Obulejo with sharp longing: with Baba by his side he would walk to the ends of the earth unafraid. Desolation sweeps over him. He turns away, gathering himself to set off alone, but then he sees Auntie gesturing to him. *Come*, her beckoning hand seems to say, *you are part of our family now*. Obulejo hesitates, then reaches for the two little girls, Jokudu and Kiden, and lifts them to their feet. They gaze at him shyly. The boys, Duku and Ladu, jump up to join their mother and sisters and their new big brother. Together they start up the hill, hurrying close behind Lege and the rest.

Tiers of low hills stretch in front of them, and further on steep mountains rise into the blinding sky. Obulejo glances back once or twice, anxiously, but can see nothing that might betray their presence, except a few areas of flattened grass, a child's hair bead caught in a thornbush, and bent shrubs and bushes still bearing the faint imprint of the bodies that had crouched in them.

His sturdy legs carry him easily up the first slope. Auntie matches his rapid pace but it is not long before the children begin to tire. The little girls start to drag on Obulejo's arms, so Obulejo leans down and scoops Kiden onto one hip and Jokudu onto the other. He staggers a moment at their combined weight, then forges on. Auntie Juan flashes him a grin of gratitude, which warms Obulejo's heart.

It is the way of his people, the way his parents have taught him to follow. Auntie had cared for him, despite having her own children to look after. Now he must help her care for the children. The fighting must not be allowed to break the old ways. He must follow Ma'di ways, to honour his family. That resolve gives Obulejo courage.

5

HOUR AFTER SCORCHING hour, Obulejo and the others hurry onwards, following Lege and the rest of the group down slopes and up hillsides, till at last they reach the edge of the dense forest. Here they halt for a few minutes. Duku and Ladu hurl themselves onto the ground and Obulejo sets Kiden down and prises Jokudu's fingers from his wrist so he can stretch his cramping limbs. After what seems only a heartbeat, everybody gets to their feet again. Auntie Juan ties her baby on more snugly and Obulejo hoists Kiden onto his back.

'Hold on tight,' he tells her. 'Pretend you're a baby monkey.'

He takes Jokudu's sticky little hand in his and off they set again. There is no time to waste.

The forest is dark and tangled with vines and creepers, but Obulejo does not hesitate. He strides swiftly, step-skip-skip-step over tangled roots, and step-slide-slip-slide-step through marshy hollows, step-gasp-climb-gasp-step up and around the contours of steep slopes, carrying one small girl and leading the other. Never stopping. Never looking back. Forging onwards. Outpacing the terror.

Obulejo has never been in thick jungle before. His ears are assaulted by the unnerving din of bustling, invisible life, a constant clamour of shrilling and trilling, swishing and clacking, a cacophony of calls, a rushing prattle of running water, creaks and flusters in the canopies of tall mahogany trees, clicks and whistles, shifts and scatters, startled shrieks and shouted alarms of innumerable hidden creatures. Equally unnerving is the deep and ominous silence that lies underneath the racket, a dense, concealing quiet in which enemies may lurk and stalking predators crouch, ready to spring.

Obulejo lost sight of Lege moments after they entered the jungle, so he keeps his eye on the retreating back of a burly man just ahead of him, and stays close. In one moment he could find himself separated from his companions by a web of dense greenness.

It is slow going in the marshy, mosquito-ridden valleys but Obulejo knows that the risk of being spotted by soldiers or tribesmen is far greater on the upper slopes.

A branch springs back suddenly. Obulejo flinches in alarm. A glint of light ahead dances and dazzles. Is it just sunlight on water or the spying eye of a concealed predator? And does that sudden upward swoop of birds warn of an unwelcome presence close by?

Breathe as quietly as possible. Push on through the terrible jungle.

Startled monkeys send scalding curses down from the treetops; before Obulejo's startled gaze a lean shadow seems to turn into a waving tree snake before metamorphosing back into a swinging vine. A tumble into a plashy creek drenches him and Jokudu and Kiden and twists his ankle cruelly.

Roots and vines snatch at his feet, and thorny bushes gouge furrows in his arms.

His heart thumping with fear, Obulejo keeps watch for the glint of spying eyes and scans the startled upward flights of birds for signals of predators approaching. He must cover the ground as rapidly as possible, before the jungle and its dangers consume him. For the meaning of his name – trouble tomorrow – has come true.

Obulejo recalls how Mama Josephina had laughed, the day she first told him the story of how he came by his name. 'All your aunties and uncles were saying to each other, "This baby will bring big trouble in the family." Trouble between myself and Mama Natalina,' she'd chuckled. 'They said, "The women will be jealous of each other," and when you were born, they named you Obulejo – trouble tomorrow. But they were wrong. Mama Natalina and I, we love each other. We help each other. We care for the children together. All one family. No trouble came, my son.'

But now, Mama Josephina's words seem hollow. Tomorrow, with worse trouble than he could ever have imagined, has him in its clutches.

The walking is interminable. Mind-numbing. Time begins to lose its shape and meaning. Minutes and hours merge.

One moment Obulejo feels that he has been fighting his way through dense thickets and navigating slippery tracks forever, fording endless streams, struggling free of thorny vines and pushing past rough-barked shrubs and trees for an eternity, and the next moment it seems he has not moved forward one inch in all that time. That he is trapped, held tight in the grip of the forest, plodding in blind circles and getting nowhere.

Hunger and thirst barely register with Obulejo. He must not hesitate or pause. He must not let exhaustion or the small girl on his back impede his progress. He pays no heed when a trickle of urine mingles with the sweat that runs down both their legs. He passes his arm across his sweaty brow and clutches Jokudu's hand more tightly as he drags her onwards. He is possessed by one desire only – to outpace the danger that pursues them.

By early afternoon some of the group are already in trouble. The smaller children are struggling to keep up; parents grow increasingly anxious for their young ones. A brief rest is called. Only the fear of losing sight of the group forces Obulejo to stop. All the while they are sitting, his fingers drum nervously on his thighs; anxious to be away again, he gets up and paces the sodden ground.

Then on again, clambering through the dappled bush with its deep shadows and blinding sun rays stippling the leaf-littered, vine-tangled floor. His mind jumps back and forth between the deep forest and the besieged town, from which, in endless replay, he once again is racing to safety.

His breath labours in his chest. He fancies he hears the sound of the Rebels' tread, and their panting progress as they gain on him. He turns sharply to catch sight of them. Nothing: just the twitch and swish and crackle and whoop of the jungle; no rifle-jab between his shoulder blades, only the slimy smear of Kiden's snotty tears on his neck.

Then everything shifts to no-time – to a place outside of time. The edges of things wobble and blur. Everything wavers and loses its shape. Where are they are going? Why?

Unsolvable puzzles. The bush disappears; the day recedes into a timeless void. An infinity of indrawn and exhaled breaths. Heat and light. Shadow and shine. Sweat and heartbeat.

The hours draw on. Obulejo notices stronger, more agile people surge ahead of the main group. Soon they disappear among the trees. He wants to rush ahead too, but he cannot leave Auntie Juan and the children behind.

When the next signal comes to stop and rest, Auntie is looking worried. The whites of her baby's eyes are tinged yellow.

'Fetch water,' Auntie Juan tells Obulejo, urgently. 'We must cool the baby's skin.'

She gives the *kere* to Obulejo and tells him where to find a spring. As Obulejo rises to obey, Auntie begins to point out to others edible bushes and foliage. Auntie knows this territory. She speaks the local language and has learned which leaves and roots and fruits are safe to eat.

Obulejo quickly returns with the brimming *kere* and Auntie bathes her baby's face. Other people straggle into the clearing. Some are carrying relatives, some are leading children or hobbling on bleeding feet. Many of the older people are shaking and grey-faced. Silent children, streaked with mud and tears, stumble forward and sink to their knees. Obulejo offers them water.

Soon people are getting ready to move on, but Auntie has other ideas. 'It is time to search for a place to hide, now,' she says. 'When darkness comes we can continue.'

Some nod agreement. Others protest.

'We are still too close to the town,' says the man whose broad back Obulejo has kept in sight since they began their trek. 'We have not come far enough yet to be safe.'

'That's right,' another man breaks in. 'We must go further if we are not to be captured.'

'There are many more miles to go,' Auntie replies, 'and to run always under the eye of the sun is not wise, if you wish to make it to the border. Besides, what helps you find your way will just as easily help others follow your tracks.'

People grumble and mutter, but most acquiesce. A few push on, mostly single men and older boys.

Obulejo is frantic at the delay. He wants to keep running forever, or until his legs give way. Until he is out of the forest and far away. Until he reaches safety.

But Auntie has spoken with authority. She has known trouble all her life and has survived it. She knows this jungle and Obulejo's survival may depend on her knowledge and experience.

'We must hide now and wait for dark,' Auntie repeats. 'Even if the Rebels are following, soldiers too must rest from time to time.'

So Obulejo and the stayers submit to Auntie's common sense. Anyway, the forest is a mind-numbing and strength-sapping soup of heat and humidity in daylight. At night, even though it is cold, they can easily warm themselves by walking.

'Come,' Auntie says. 'I know a place.'

They follow her along a watercourse and down a steeply wooded incline. The damp red soil is thick with layers of rotting vegetation, and soft underfoot; it muffles their footsteps. They struggle with the clumps of reeds, tangled overhanging branches and viciously thorny vines that grab and clutch at legs and shoulders, but which also may offer secure hiding places.

Obulejo helps Auntie settle her children into the leafy embrace of a spreading bush then searches for a hiding place for himself and the little girl he carries. He is grateful for the company, although Kiden has not uttered a sound since first being hoisted onto Obulejo's back.

People quickly conceal themselves. The forest swallows them up as though they had never been there at all.

6

OBULEJO HASTILY DIGS a shallow burrow for himself and Kiden, under a large heap of decaying leaves and reeds beside the rushing stream.

It is a good hiding place. Well chosen, he thinks, with a small swell of pride. It will keep them safe. He lowers himself into the hollow he has scooped out. Good, there are no scorpions or spiders. Once installed in the hideout, he pulls reeds and fronds over their heads. There is plenty of room to breathe and they can keep a lookout through the gaps in the undergrowth.

Before he has fully relaxed, a warning flashes in his mind. A memory of his grandfather saying, 'A wise Ma'di never camps close to a river, for riverbanks are a favourite haunt of snakes.' How could Obulejo have forgotten? He should have followed Auntie and hidden close to her. Now he has led himself and Auntie's little daughter into great danger.

Only once has Obulejo witnessed the death throes of a person bitten by a mamba, and he has never forgotten the bloated limbs and contorted face. He must get himself and Kiden out of here! But what if they are spotted leaving and his rash action leads to everyone else being discovered?

He sits there sweating. Each slight movement or teasing sound – the shusshing of grass or the rasp of twigs against each other, the tilt and flutter of leaves and branches overhead, even the lilting movement of large butterflies in flight – shouts MAMBA! Obulejo can picture the serpent slithering closer with deadly intent – ready to strike.

Oh, the shame of having a child's death on his hands! He, who has always been so conscientious about protecting young ones given into his care. The impulse to break cover and rush deeper into the forest, dragging the child with him, is almost irresistible. But just as Obulejo is about to fling off the reed covering, he hears a distant rat-tat-tatting. Gunfire? A bird pecking? He cannot tell. All he knows is that he must stay put, even if a thousand snakes lurk nearby.

He strains his ears and stills his breath a moment, then breathes out carefully as each new alarm proves to be nothing more than the normal busy life of the forest around him. Birds shriek and whistle in the treetops. Unseen creatures rootle in the undergrowth. Leaves swish and crackle and clatter. Glimpses of dancing shadows startle his watchful eyes.

He tries to pray but the words won't come. '*Opi Yesu, Opi Yesu,*' he mouths, silently, over and over, 'Lord Jesus, Lord Jesus,' and can get no further.

Finally, as the shadows begin to lengthen and the heat of the day starts to abate, Obulejo detects a movement that at first makes his heart race, and then sends his spirits soaring. Little more than the flicker of a dark hand at first, quickly followed by the glimpse of a body partly obscured in the dappled light. It is one of their group, a grizzled man whose muddy trousers with their torn fringes Obulejo instantly recognises. Obulejo watches intently as the man lowers his bleeding calves into the stream and splashes water over them. He pushes the reeds aside and lifts Kiden out of the hollow, then scrambles after her. He greets the man, and follows him along a muddy track to where others are assembling. He and Kiden have survived the first day of the journey, in spite of his foolish mistake in choosing the riverbank as a hideout.

More people silently emerge in the gathering dusk, and make ready to resume their march.

Obulejo hears a low moan.

'Mama,' Kiden whispers.

Obulejo scans the clearing.

The moaning continues. Obulejo rushes to a low bush close by, parts the branches and peers in. The boys and Jokudu are clutching their mother's skirts, while Auntie rocks her baby in her arms. The baby's face is grey and still.

A whisper runs through the group. 'The child is deceased.'

People gather round Auntie and clasp her hand in sympathy. They speak quietly to her, whispering prayers for her and her baby.

'*Baba ama ata bua rii*, our Father who art in heaven, gather this child into your arms and comfort her mother.'

'Always it is the defenceless who must bear the greatest cost of war,' Auntie whispers, tears spilling down her face.

Three men quietly begin to dig a grave and others gather rocks to place over it, to safeguard Keji's body against jungle predators and scavengers.

Obulejo watches as Auntie bathes her baby's body, wraps it in a cloth and places the small bundle in the grave. A few more prayers are whispered before the soil is tamped down and weighted with rocks. Mothers clutch their children close.

Auntie gestures to Obulejo: *give me my child.* He reluctantly passes Kiden to her. Auntie clutches her daughter to her chest. Duku and Ladu put their arms round their sisters and pat their mother's bowed shoulders.

Auntie Juan turns to the silent onlookers. 'I thank you for your kindness to my baby,' she says, 'but now you must move on, quickly.'

'What this woman says is true,' a short plump woman mutters. 'We cannot stay here and risk being caught.'

But how can they leave a tiny baby all by herself in the jungle? She should be back home, in the village, close to her family, so they can look after her.

But Auntie Juan and the short woman are right. They must set off again immediately. *Why did Auntie say 'you', not 'we'?* Obulejo wonders. People start to move off. Obulejo reaches for Kiden, to hoist her onto his back again, but Auntie shakes her head. 'My children must stay by my side.'

Obulejo's heart sinks. He has become so used to Kiden's warm little body plastered to his back. With her to care for he doesn't feel so alone. But after the loss of her youngest child, Auntie must be desperate to keep her other children with her. He tries not to let his face betray his feelings. It is right for the child to be with her family, and it removes the burden from his back. He will be able to travel more quickly now, make better time. But he will miss that small, warm, trusting weight, the reassuring beat of another heart close to his.

The ache for his own family intensifies. Their absence presses more sharply in his chest.

But he must keep walking – further and further away from them. Out of reach of what he most longs for. Out of reach of what he fears is pursuing him.

The next minute Obulejo's world tilts again.

'I will go back,' Auntie tells him.

'No!'

Auntie puts a gentle hand on his forearm. 'I must,' she repeats. 'I have lost my husband already, in this war, and now my baby. My parents I left behind in Torit, and now I must go back and find them. I will throw myself on the mercy of the Rebels. They are countrymen. Surely they will not harm us.'

Obulejo stares dumbly as Auntie turns and gathers her children for the journey back.

'I cannot lose another of my children,' she adds quietly.

Four small children and one woman – how will they accomplish such a journey alone? Obulejo must go with them. But the memory of the guns, the screaming, the soldiers' threats stops him in his tracks. Maybe the Rebels will spare Auntie, but they certainly won't spare him. He'll be forced to join the Rebel army, or he may even be shot. He has no choice. He must keep going, and try to get to the border. Yet how can he leave this woman to struggle back through the jungle on her own, when she has cared for him like a mother?

She will not be on her own, it turns out. Others are hurrying to join her. Older people, other women with children. *Have they decided to take their chances with the Rebels, too*, Obulejo wonders, *or have they just no more strength to push on through the jungle?*

The moment of parting comes too soon. Those determined to keep heading east begin to move, and Obulejo reluctantly bids Auntie farewell and hurries after them. He looks back only once before pushing aside clinging vines and tendrils and plunging into the cloying darkness. The jungle soon closes around him. He can no longer hear the footsteps of the retreating group. His new-made little family is lost to him, perhaps forever.

He is a boy alone, without family, once again.

7

ALL THAT LONG night the fugitives walk and scramble in virtual silence through dense jungle.

Heavy-hearted, Obulejo plods on. The urgency of his need to find refuge still thrums in his chest as insistently as ever, but as each step forward takes him further from Auntie and her children he wonders if Auntie was right, whether he should have gone back with her. At least she knows the territory. But in spite of these thoughts, his feet keep moving steadily eastward.

Being in the forest in the dark is perilous. So many predators hunt by night. But Obulejo is glad of the cover of darkness. When he trips over roots, gets caught up in unseen branches and tangled among barbed vines, he extricates himself as quickly as possible, sucks his torn fingers and presses on.

The trekkers stop twice, and only briefly, to gather gourds, bulrushes and tufted wild grasses. Obulejo eats only when prompted, impatiently gnawing the pulpy end of a bulrush stem, then wrapping the rest in his shirt for later. His legs twitch to be underway and when the leaders head off he strides after them immediately, intent on putting as much distance between himself and the Rebels as he can, as quickly as possible. He tries to banish thoughts of Mama and Baba as they arise. His survival depends on not looking backwards, not thinking about what he has lost, but pressing on, and staying close to these strangers he is with, people facing the same peril.

It is because of people like Lege, like Auntie, that he has got this far. He prays that Auntie will find her way home and that she and her children will be safe. He thinks of poor little Keji, lying alone in the forest, and hopes she is now safe in heaven.

Thanks to God for those who know this forest. On them his safety depends. On his own there is no way he could find a way through the bewildering proliferation of rivers and thickets, criss-crossed with animal tracks, sharp grasses, barbed leaves, tangled branches and a thousand traps for the unwary, not to mention leopards, hyenas, *lore* and venomous creatures like mambas. Alone, he would have been forced to turn back and surrender himself to the Rebels. Every time he momentarily loses the sound and sight of those in front, the darkness seems deeper and unseen dangers press more closely. He cannot breathe easily until he catches up.

He trusts their knowledge as Auntie had trusted him to take care of Kiden. It is the way of his people; the young belong to the whole tribe and the responsibility of caring for them and for each other rests on everyone.

How then has hatred and killing come about, among the people? What makes tribe turn against tribe? Will there ever be an end to it?

All of a sudden the thick darkness is torn apart by a blood-curdling scream. Obulejo stops dead in his tracks. The jungle explodes into a cacophony of panicked scurries and shrieks as terrified birds and creatures flee. A sobbing scream rises higher and higher in pitch.

Someone crashes into him and he is tumbled to the ground and soon buried in a press of bodies. He pushes and struggles beneath a pile of arms and legs until he is able to get to his feet.

'Leopard!' someone shouts, and the jungle is full of the thunder of running feet.

The terrified scream continues, then trails off to a dreadful silence.

Obulejo charges along with the others, back the way they came, stumbling, slipping, falling as he scrambles to escape this new horror that has come upon them

'Who has been taken?' he shouts.

A babble of answers. Nobody knows for sure.

What is certain is that the victim is no longer alive. Obulejo's ears catch the sound of hyenas barking; already the scavengers must be moving in close to the kill, waiting for a chance to feast on the prey.

The unsuspecting victim must have made his way along, not knowing the danger he was in, while on a branch above his head a leopard crouched, ready to spring.

Obulejo must not think of that now. Just go!

Almost blind with terror, he crashes through the jungle with the rest of the fleeing people.

When they finally regather, hundreds of yards from the scene of the attack, more people decide they too will try to make their way back home. For them, this latest disaster is the last straw. For Obulejo the choice seems impossible. To go on is to risk death from wild animals. To go back carries the same risk from soldiers.

The man taken by the leopard is Obale. A swift, strong, young man.

'If he has fallen prey, then how can others, weaker, slower, hope to survive?' an old man says.

Lege speaks then. 'The leopard will be busy with its kill. We must take a wide path around him and move on quickly.'

He does not speak of Obale, and Obulejo understands why. To dwell on the horror will weaken their resolve to move on.

Sombrely, the group splits into two. Some turn back, while the others, Obulejo among them, file after Lege.

The nightmare continues.

The first signs of dawn begin to lighten the night sky before those in the lead come to a halt.

Obulejo is both relieved and alarmed when they stop. His eyes sting and his breath labours in his chest, but despite his aching legs and leaden feet he continues to pace restlessly.

'Hurry!' he feels like shouting at the leaders. 'While we stand here talking, another leopard may be stalking us.'

Others in the group voice the same urgency. 'We should not stop yet,' many contend. 'We must go on until the sun is high.'

Some younger men decide to press on, and quickly disappear into the surrounding forest. Others, especially older people and those with children, begin to search for hiding places.

Obulejo steers clear of the riverbank this time and finds refuge in among the roots of a gigantic spreading tree, covering himself with its broad fallen leaves. Once or twice he imagines he hears the rumbly purr of a leopard overhead but he dares not risk prising a gap in his canopy of leaves to find out. He just hunkers down lower and tries to still his breath to an imperceptible ripple. A long, hot, lonely day passes. It is hard to sit still and do nothing. He recalls Auntie explaining to the impatient ones, 'A day in hiding is both a day lost and a day gained.' He wishes she were still with them. And little Kiden, how can she walk all the way home, perhaps into even worse danger?

At the end of the day, a few more people announce they are turning back.

'The trek has taxed my mother's strength too greatly,' one woman says, her eyes downcast. 'I am afraid she will die if we continue.'

'I am at breaking point,' her mother adds.

A murmur of sympathy comes from some in the group.

'To die in the jungle is a foolish thing,' an older man agrees. 'I'll take my chance with the Rebels.'

Others chime in.

'A known peril is preferable to an unknown fate.'

'Better punishment at home, even death, than being mauled by jungle beasts.'

Obulejo shivers. Perhaps it was a leopard he heard from his hiding place, or a cheetah. Maybe a lion that had wandered into the undergrowth. There are terrible animals in the jungle; look what they are capable of!

'Foolish people,' Lege says, 'have you forgotten already how many have been killed in this war and the last? If you return, do you think the Rebels will spare you?'

But the deserters cannot be persuaded. They turn their faces homeward and begin to retrace their steps.

Obulejo stares after them, torn between the urge to rush onwards with the bold young men and the longing to head back home with the deserters. By now, his father may be looking for him. And if the others get back and he is not with them, Baba will think the worst. But when the last homeward-bound person disappears into the shadows, Obulejo readies himself to march on, further away from home. Hasn't he always followed the bidding of the elders? However much his panic tells him, 'Run back!' he will abide by the decisions of the leaders.

Obulejo mentally counts the absentees. Auntie and her children and those who went back with her, those who turned back after the leopard attack, and today five more. But that still doesn't account for everyone. Some of the younger men seem to be missing. And a few senior men and women. Some have gone on ahead. Others may have taken a wrong turn and got lost. Or been eaten. Obulejo dares not dwell on this possibility. He must focus on the next step, the next stream to be forded, the next thicket to get through, the next hill to climb. Each step will bring him closer to Kenya; if only he can get through the jungle and avoid capture.

The group continues to pick its wary way through the forest. They stop only to scoop up handfuls of water from streams. Everyone is mosquito-bitten, scratched and torn, but no one complains. They have been lucky so far. Except for poor little Keji, and for Obale's dreadful end. Obulejo shudders at the memory. When will they ever get through this jungle?

When hyenas bark and whine, Obulejo is filled with rage and disgust. He loathes these opportunistic scavengers. The smaller children shiver and shrink against their parents' legs, their eyes big and round, but they utter no cries. They hurry to keep step with the adults; to be left behind is the most terrifying prospect of all.

The walkers make the most of the cover that darkness offers. Cold as it is once the sun goes down, footsore, thirsty and increasingly hungry as they become, their feet torn and blistered, their arms and faces scratched and scarred from encounters with thorns and rough bushes, they nevertheless welcome the dark, particularly when the moon hides its face and they can press on more quickly in greater safety.

As soon as birds wake and before the sun rises, hot and stupefying, the daily scramble begins for thickets and hollows to hide in.

One time, Obulejo parts the branches of a thick bush to discover a worried mother with two terrified children crouching beside her. Another time he unearths a student of his own age buried under leaves in a hollow he had marked out as a possible hideout.

Those who can, snatch some sleep during the heat of the day, using soft leaves as a bed and a shirt or cloth for coverings, or leaves and grass if they have nothing else. They sleep silently; no snores or coughs or even a whimper from an infant betray their presence.

Day follows day of silent, breathless waiting. Night follows night of limping progress eastwards. Towards capture or freedom? Obulejo wonders. But he cannot afford to think too hard.

There is no turning back now.

8

THE RISKS OF travelling in another tribe's territory without permission are great. Obulejo shudders to think of the possible consequences if they are discovered. Will they be shot on sight? Turned over to the Rebels and forced to join the war? He has heard many stories of boy soldiers trained to slaughter even their own families. There is no way he could ever harm his family. And yet, others like him have been forced to commit these terrible deeds.

He keeps a close eye on the aunties' skirts brushing through the tall undergrowth ahead and the men clawing back vines, and he wills himself to take heart and keep his courage high.

The familiar certainties that once sustained him – home, family, school – have been swept away, just as the driving rains regularly used to crash down at home, sweep anything in their paths before them and transform placid rivers into foaming torrents.

He is beset by questions with no answers: is freedom ever to be his? Where is safety? Is the life he knew lost to him forever? He thrusts the questions aside. His attention must remain on the next step, the next rest stop, the next hiding place, the next day's shelter.

His whole body aches, but there is no time or place for rest. For a few seconds he fantasises that he will lie down in peace, sleep the night through and wake to find all this has been just a nightmare; that the new day that greets him holds maths and geography, grammar and games and spelling, cooking the evening meal, homework, reciting prayers and falling once more into peaceful sleep. A dangerous fantasy. It makes him weak with longing. Tears push at his eyelids.

One question torments Obulejo. Had his father not been an educated man, with a high-up job that took the family far from the Ma'di lands, would this desperate situation have come upon him? Could a different life, a kinder fate, have been his, with no armies or guns or fear?

He knows such thoughts are not helpful but like the tongue worrying a sore tooth his mind forever returns to them.

How many days have they been walking? Obulejo loses track.

He is moving like an automaton now, mechanically putting one foot in front of the other. Relentlessly going forward, step by step, ignoring the pain from his many gashes.

Darkness or light, heat or cold, storm or sun barely register with him.

But what does register is that the group is breaking up, bit by bit. People are beginning to walk in smaller groups. The strong and whole move on ahead, while those with desperate injuries lag behind. The children are becoming gaunt and grey-skinned.

'Leaves and wild fruit are not enough to nourish them,' Lege admits to their anxious mothers. 'They need milk and good maize porridge.'

One night, another baby dies in its mother's arms. For the second time a grave is dug, and prayers are chanted.

Just after nightfall the next evening Obulejo emerges from his hiding place ready for the night's trek only to find that he is alone. His heart clutches in panic. Surely the others have not left him to die? Tears run down his face as he searches frantically for their tracks. Which way to run? He can't figure it out. The moon has not yet risen. The dark trees press close. He is alone in the whispering, clattering, swishing, shrieking, clamouring jungle.

Then a thought comes to him. He drops to the peaty forest floor and presses his ear against the earth, straining to catch the sound of a footfall. Nothing. Disappointment knocks the breath out of him. Despair whispers to him to just bury his face in the mud, stop up his mouth and nostrils and his ordeal will be over. He will rest with the ancestors.

Almost, he gives in to the idea. Almost, but not quite. He suddenly sees himself from the outside. His father's son, lying in the mud, a snivelling child. Preparing to throw away the gift of life given by God as if it were worthless. Bringing shame to his parents, to the older brothers, the uncles, the whole clan. Never!

Obulejo rises to his knees, struggles upright and brushes off the clinging mud. Not knowing which direction to take, he starts to walk anyway. Perhaps he could find a river and follow its course. Or climb a hill – no, he will see nothing from its summit in the black night, and unseen watchers may spot him.

He blunders along blindly. More than once he is caught in the vicious tendrils of the lawyer vine. As he tears himself loose, bleeding, he is certain that invisible predators are padding silently towards him, ready to spring. But he must keep going, and he does, hour after desperate hour.

Then he notices that the jungle is beginning to thin out. Tall trees still form dense canopies overhead but there don't seem to be so many entangling vines and hanging creepers now. Obulejo has no idea where he is but at least the going is easier. Almost as soon as he has that thought, he realises that the danger of being seen will be much greater in more open bush.

He hesitates on the edge of a clearing. Dare he risk crossing it? He glances up at the sky. The gibbous moon swims bright and gloating, ready to give him away. He waits and listens. About to take a chance to flit silently to the cover of the nearby trees, he fancies he sees a flicker of movement. Beast? Soldier? Tribesman? He shrinks back into the shadows. Stands as still as a boulder. His breath comes in shallow bursts. He clamps his mouth shut, to muffle the sound. Listens. Waits.

Nothing. He must have imagined it. Slowly and sound-lessly he skirts the edges of the clearing, melts into the shadows – and stiffens as a hand covers his mouth, his arms are pinned back and a tall, strong body clamps itself to his.

Obulejo struggles soundlessly.

'Hey, Ma'di boy, hey,' hisses a voice in his ear.

'*Ita wadru wen?*' another voice taunts, in Sudanese Arabic. 'Where did you get lost?'

Obulejo's knees buckle. Tears prick at his eyelids. He is finished!

Next minute Obulejo is swung round to face his attackers. Two young men stand under the moon, grinning. They are

older and taller than Obulejo, but he recognises them immediately. Opio and Otim – Acholi lads. And the one holding
him is Laku, a tall Kuku boy. They'd been part of the group
fleeing through the jungle.

'What's the idea of ambushing me, baboons?' he demands,
his insulting words covering tears of relief.

Several wide grins flash; several sets of white teeth shine in
the moonlight.

'You're easy prey,' Laku says.

'Easier than tracking game,' Otim adds.

'Little monkey can't see past its tail,' Opio teases.

Annoyed, Obulejo strains furiously in his captor's grip.

'Easy, little *orogu*,' Laku chuckles. 'I'll set you free if you
promise not to bite.'

'Or spit,' Otim adds, and a hissing laugh whistles from
between his front teeth.

Obulejo's rage cools quickly in the joy of finding himself
no longer alone. And when the boys invite him to join their
group he is overcome with relief. The night ahead may prove
as long and arduous as the ones before, but it will seem far
easier in the company of these three.

How quickly the time passes, with companions. The
going is easier now they have emerged from the thick bush.
Run, Obulejo, run! is the drum-beat of his every in-breath and
out-breath, and of each step he takes. As he runs he remembers
his childhood – the times he's raced to obey Moini's call, or
dashed to the river to bathe before the day's lessons so he does
not arrive late at school.

Now he is running to save his skin.

All night the four boys lope across scrubby plains full of
spindly bushes and clumped grasses. The jungle is behind

them, its dense undergrowth and tangled vines no longer impeding their progress. But without its trickling streams and moist and dripping leaves they can run all night without finding water. They search for soaks, but find none. Their next drinking water is wrung drop by reluctant drop from early-morning dew.

This place is so different from home, Obulejo thinks, gazing around him as daylight begins to tint the sky. No palm-leaf caves cleverly constructed by *cwa*, weaver birds, no flooding rivers, no waving savannah grasses; the dun-coloured grass is short and sparse. Termite mounds stand like sentinels in the dusty landscape.

'Toposa territory,' Otim tells Obulejo. 'We must take care they don't see us.'

'They guard their cattle with rifles,' Opio says.

Laku mimes being shot. Otim and Opio giggle; Obulejo flinches.

He takes in the buzz of insects, the acrid smell of dust in the nostrils, the dry immensity of sun-baked earth and the straggle of low thornbush and clumps of acacia. He thinks of his lush mountain village and does not envy the Toposa their pitiless land. But he must count his blessings as the holy fathers have taught him. God has spared him. He is still free.

Obulejo has only the vaguest idea of where he is. Close to the Kenyan border, he hopes. All he knows to do – all any of them know – is to keep moving in the direction of the rising sun, for that way lies the border and safety. How far they have come or how far they still have to go is uncertain.

Here in this dry land, death stalks the boys at every turn. Obulejo feels its hot breath on his neck, its bite at his heels, senses its presence in the circling vultures overhead and hears its banshee shrieks in the dust-filled winds that flay the broken plains.

It is here they must outrun death.

But right now the sun is swinging higher in the sky, and they must find safe hiding places for the day.

Opio, Otim and Laku set off at a run towards a grove of acacia bushes. *Too obvious*, Obulejo thinks. He looks around frantically. Where to hide? He spots a group of termite hills a little way off, and rushes towards them. It's his flimsiest hiding place yet, but it will have to do. No time to look for a more secure place. He scoops out a hollow in the shade of the biggest mound and flings himself into it, scrabbling dusty earth over himself as fast as he can.

The north–south alignment of the termite hill will save him from the worst of the midday sun, but will his shelter hide him from the sharp eyes of the Toposa herders, or from the guns of the Rebels?

He envies the termites, secure inside their fortress. If only he were like them, safe in his home, and surrounded by family.

9

ALL DAY LONG Obulejo's muscles brace themselves for flight. His lips are parched and in his mouth is the acrid anticipation of imminent capture.

Late in the afternoon he falls into a restless sleep, waking abruptly a short while later. The sun is almost below the horizon, and the heat is diminishing. Obulejo cautiously emerges from his hiding place and heads off in the direction of his companions. He reaches the clump of acacia bushes and scouts around for a while, but can find no sign of Opio, Otim or Laku. The ground is brushed smooth: perhaps they have concealed their tracks. He dare not call out to them, in case someone less welcome answers his shout. They must have set off earlier, expecting him to catch them up. He turns his back to the setting sun and sets off to the east.

For the first few hours he assumes they are ahead of him, just out of sight, and that soon he will come upon them slinking along in the shadows. He quickens his pace to a swift, smooth stride. Fights down the thought that older, stronger, taller than he, they may have outpaced him.

What if they have just left him behind? He'll never catch up.

Panic grabs him. Then blinding rage. Why didn't they wake him?

Perhaps they've been captured.

Why must it be like this? Why must he find companions only to have them snatched away again? Is this to be his new life – new friends made one moment and snatched away the next?

All he knows for certain is that he is on Toposa lands and that the Toposa do not welcome intruders. If they discover him, the whole terrifying journey will have been for nothing. To have come all this way from the guns and soldiers and nearly perish from hunger and thirst and then to be captured and turned over to the Rebels – it's too horrible to contemplate. But at any moment it may happen.

Like a bird caught in a snare, frantically beating its wings, twisting and turning, Obulejo struggles against the possibility of failure, of defeat, of capture, even as he cannot imagine how to avoid them.

All night long he walks alone, with never a glimpse of Opio, Otim or Laku. He listens for sounds of cattle lowing, for the sight of campfires, and carefully skirts any areas where he spots movement or evidence of tribesmen.

At last the new day dawns and once again he must set about the task of finding a hiding place. He selects a tussock of grass and slumps down into it.

Sitting in his skimpy hiding place, he clasps his dusty arms around his chest, feeling the beat of his wildly racing heart. His legs tremble. Now the tribesmen will come rushing out of the bush, brandishing spears or rifles. Now!

Dried grass stems rasp and clatter, then fall silent. Are they waiting, hiding, ready to strike? He jerks around, ready to meet a barrage of spears, or the barrel of a rifle, only to see nothing but heat waves shimmering across the bone-dry plains.

But still, he cannot rid himself of the feeling that he is being held in the glare of unseen eyes. He tries to ignore the feeling, but it persists, till he is shaking with tension, consumed by the desire to get away – not just crouch here and become a hunter's target.

He can bear it no longer. He must break cover. Hurl himself at the guns, if necessary. Anything but lie here and wait to be picked off like a foolish dove.

When barely discernible snappings and rustlings approach Obulejo's hiding place he readies himself for the end. Dry stalks part and a face – not a gun – thrusts itself through. Obulejo jerks backwards. His heart thuds faster than the dance drums.

'Ai-eeeeh!'

'Ai-eeeeh!' comes the equally startled response, the other face as shocked as his own.

'Ai-eeh! Ochan!'

'Obulejo, my friend!'

The tall, gawky Acholi steps forward and clasps Obulejo's arm. Obulejo has suffered such desperate loneliness, and now God has sent him a friend. Someone from his old life; from St Xavier's and the mountain village.

Obulejo and Ochan dance around one another like puppies, slapping each other's shoulders, giddy with relief.

A second boy steps forward, then another and another: three more Acholi boys.

Ochan quickly introduces him, and from that moment Obulejo is part of a group again.

This time he determines he will not let his companions out of his sight for a moment. There are risks in travelling in a group, but the advantages are far greater. A silent song of thanks rises to his lips – for his new companions and for all who have helped him on the journey.

So, now they are five. Akere and Ayella, who are brothers, Loding, Ochan and Obulejo. Four Acholi boys and one Ma'di, but with a shared single goal: to reach Kenya and safety. They will do it together, God willing. The boys will stay together from now on, they promise each other. They'll share food and water, hunt together and help each other, as they make their way through Toposa territory, past the endless clumps of thornbush and umbrella trees, and onwards to shimmering horizons.

The going is tough. They find very little to eat, and their searches for water most often end in disappointment. But one evening Obulejo spots a familiar-looking tree amid the slanted shadows. As he gets closer he sees that there are still a few lemon-shaped *oba* suspended from its thorny branches. He carefully plucks the fruit and hurries to rejoin his companions.

They greet him happily.

'The hunter returns!' Loding says.

'Bearing big game,' Ayella teases.

Ochan smiles his thanks as Obulejo tips his share of the *oba* into his friend's hands. On their next rest stop the boys suck eagerly on the sour fruit, their faces contorting in grimaces. Refreshed, they are able to continue.

Then Akere has an opportunity to provide for the group. He points to a milling cloud of tiny flying creatures, which they follow to a dry hollow where sweet crusted sugar is stored. Quickly they rob the cache and stuff themselves with sweetness as the agitated owners swarm angrily about their heads.

'Lucky these ones don't sting,' Akere says.

'Not like bees and hornets,' Ayella says, ruefully.

His brother laughs. 'Remember that time when you were small and you poked a hornets' nest?'

'Ai-eeh, I couldn't sit down for a week!'

The boys grin.

The sugar is not enough to satisfy their growling stomachs, but all are grateful to Akere. By now they are used to being hungry. What Obulejo finds more unsettling than the feeling of emptiness in his belly is the gnawing rodent of terror eating away at his vitals, day and night, awake or asleep. It won't let him rest; it keeps him constantly vigilant. He can see it's the same for the others. They are all alert, watchful, at the slightest disturbance ready to leap up and run.

The search for food is constant. Ayella proves himself adept with a snare. From time to time he manages to capture small birds. These he shares with the other boys. The bones of each bird are soon stripped of flesh and sucked dry.

But it is Loding who has the biggest triumph. He finds a soak. For the first time since they left the jungle, the boys are able to drink their fill. When their thirst is sated, they rest a while under the spreading branches of a shady tree.

Akere groans in relief.

The others turn to Loding and salute him. Loding swells with pride.

'My friend, you have saved our lives,' Ochan says. 'Thanks to God.'

Ochan's only contribution so far has been a handful of wild fruits, but the others know he will contribute as he can. They are all in this together.

So far they have been lucky, lucky, lucky. They have pushed through jungle and grassland, and so far not come upon Toposa or Rebel. And thanks to God they have strong legs to keep walking, keen ears to listen for danger and friendly companions to share the journey with.

Strive harder, remain strong and stay with Ochan and the other Acholi boys, that is Obulejo's resolve. He refuses to give in to pain or exhaustion. He heeds the voice inside that tells him, *Move! Now! Go!* And somehow, his body is able to keep obeying what his mind and heart demand of it.

On the third day of their travels together, Ochan says, 'For two days we have seen no dust from cattle herds. I believe we are coming closer to the border.'

Obulejo begins to allow himself a small portion of hope that they may get through to safety after all.

10

OCHAN IS IN the lead when, high above them, they hear planes roar and dip. Lokichogio air base! They are getting near the border! They must proceed with great caution now. The troops in this area will be alert and dangerous and will show no mercy.

The boys take a wide detour, keeping away from roads and any sound of military activity. They strain to catch any sign of human habitation – barking dogs, smoke rising, meandering cattle with a keen-eyed herder in tow.

Suddenly, as they are skirting a patch of thornbushes, Ochan stops dead, turns, signals urgently to the others. Before they can react, they are surrounded by a scowling bunch of men, scantily clad, with rifles slung across their shoulders. Toposa! All gabbling, shouting in a menacing way. There is nowhere to hide, no time to run. Trained from childhood to herd and chase cattle, the Toposa are legendary runners. What the boys have dreaded has come to pass. Now they will be delivered into the hands of the Rebels by these herders.

Obulejo stares in horror as a torrent of angry questions is flung at them; accusations, threats, demands. The boys turn their palms upward, plead their innocence in Arabic, Acholi and Ma'di.

'*Anama adu*,' Ochan says in Arabic. 'I'm not an enemy.'

The men's faces glower threateningly.

Akere swaps to Acholi. '*An latin kwan.* I'm a student.'

'*Ma bara sukutodri*,' Obulejo echoes, in Ma'di.

But no glimmer of understanding appears on the scowling faces of the herders.

The boys catch each other's eyes. They are outnumbered. And they stand no chance against full-grown men with rifles. The fastest runner cannot outpace a bullet.

The herders signal the boys to move, and jostle their captives forward in a rapid forced march across the baking plains.

As they approach a more wooded area, built-up structures become visible among the trees. A Toposa cattle camp? A Rebel outpost? Obulejo tries not to think of the possible fate that awaits them. Execution. Enforced military service. Death, at the hands of the Rebels.

But then a small, insistent voice rises inside him, like a bird piping shrilly over and over through the mist of fear, 'I want to live. I want to live.'

'Stop!'

The sudden shout halts them in their tracks. They glance wildly at each other. A row of rifles is pointed at their chests.

Rebel soldiers.

'Who goes?' The challenge comes in guttural Arabic.

The boys stand transfixed. Struck dumb. Unable to respond. The Toposa herders step aside. Their work is done. The soldiers will deal with the trespassers.

'*Adis!*' The Arabic word for lentil.

Silence.

'*Adis!*' This time, the challenge comes with a more aggressive edge.

The boys glance at each other in desperation. This must be the signal for them to reply with the password.

'*Adis!*'

This is it, Obulejo thinks.

But instead of bullets, questions are fired at them, in heavily accented Arabic.

'Who are you people?'

'What are you doing on Toposa land?'

'Why did you leave your homes?'

'Why have you come here?'

'Where are you going?'

'Are you with the government?'

'Are your parents soldiers?'

'Are they with the government?'

'Tell us or we will shoot you, pitiful dogs.'

There is no time to think, no time to dissemble. Ochan answers for them all.

'We don't know where we are.'

'We left the war.'

'We ran away from the fighting.'

'We aren't with the government.'

'We are students, sir.'

The boys huddle together and stare at the cracked soil.

Obulejo's head starts to spin. He tries to unglue his tongue. If he does not speak soon, they will beat him. These men want answers and they want them fast. But he is mute. At first he is grateful that Ochan has the presence of mind to respond promptly. But then he thinks, *what if Ochan betrays us to save himself?* He could tell the soldiers that Obulejo is the son of an educated man who holds an important position, and secure his own release in return for Obulejo's life. Everyone knows about the reprisals against educated men in positions of authority. About children forced at gunpoint to betray their families. About the beatings and torture.

Obulejo's face grows hot. What would *he* do, in Ochan's position? He wants to believe he'd stand by his friends. But would he have the courage? He slides a sideways glance in Ochan's direction. Ochan is standing passive but unflinching, a blank expression on his face. He does not meet the soldiers' eyes, but keeps his gaze lowered.

What will he do?

Whatever Ochan does and whatever vengeance the soldiers wreak, Obulejo knows he is powerless. The hope that was beginning to take root in his heart is now just a discarded calabash lying in the corner of a compound, waiting for a sweeper to gather its broken shards and cart them to the trash heap to be burned.

Obulejo finds his voice at last. 'He is telling the truth, sir. We are students.'

'Very early in the morning,' Ochan continues, 'fighting started, so we ran.'

The boys indicate their scarred legs. Surely the soldiers must see what they are saying is true.

But the soldiers aren't convinced.

'Liars! Liars! You are spies! Who sent you to spy on us?'

Once again, the bitter taste of impending death begins to sour Obulejo's throat.

'Tell us who you are! Tell us why you are spying on us! Tell us now!'

Abuse rains down on them. The boys stand helpless.

Finally the soldiers bind the boys' hands with thick thongs and herd them towards an unroofed enclosure fenced with interlaced thornbushes. They are handed over to a soldier with two stripes on his sleeves. A corporal. This man is even worse than the sentries.

'You were sent here to spy!' the corporal shouts.

And no matter how many times the boys deny it, no matter how they plead and protest that they are only schoolboys, the corporal spits accusations and abuse in their faces with increasing frenzy. All five are soon shaking with terror.

'Lock them up,' the corporal orders, 'and make sure they do not escape.'

A guard wearing a tattered version of the Rebel uniform gestures with his weapon. The boys shuffle forward.

'Understand this,' the corporal roars behind them, 'you belong to us now! You will fight with us for the liberation of Sudan or die!'

The guard grinds a hefty metal door open, hurries the boys inside. They hear the gate clang shut and a latch being fastened.

Inside are twenty or so men huddled in silent groups around the walls.

Obulejo crouches in the dirt with his friends.

Everything good gets smashed, wiped away, he thinks bitterly. *Guns and threats and violence rule the world.*

He remembers the Bible story of the man whose house was full of demons that tormented him day and night; the man begs for the demons to be cast out and when Jesus does this the grateful man sweeps and cleans his empty house. But even while he is still rejoicing, a crowd of new demons, a thousand times stronger and more ferocious than the first lot, comes roaring in to recapture the house.

Demons now come roaring in on Obulejo. Their hot breath scorches his throat; their strong claws tear at his vitals.

They taunt him with visions of hideous tortures, and his own painful death. He has no strength to call for help or to cast them out. The demons have him in their power.

'*Adis*!' they jeer. 'Now you are ours!'

'You will die! Your family will never know what became of you!'

Obulejo hunkers lower, hands crossed over his head to block out the tumult. But the demons never let up. They dance their triumph over his bowed head.

Is this the end?

Tears slither down his knees and pool on the dusty earth.

Hours later, when he finally is able once again to pay attention, Obulejo finds they are in a fully equipped Rebel camp manned by seasoned soldiers who are obviously angry that they have been assigned to guard a miserable rabble of prisoners.

Meagre rations are brought to the other prisoners, but the boys are given nothing that day.

Akere and Ayella curl up like puppies and fall asleep – or pretend to – holding each other tightly. Loding agitatedly paces the perimeter of their prison. But Ochan and Obulejo just sit, knees to chests, saying nothing.

Ochan seems steady and unperturbed, but perhaps he has simply done as Obulejo has – taken his mind and spirit out of this barren prison and sent it back to familiar places, back to the gardens, to the banks of rippling streams, to the firesides in the compounds at night with families gathered, where the elders tell stories in the flickering light and the girls by the grain houses send sideways flirty glances from under downcast eyelashes at boys they fancy.

No, those memories are too painful. It is better to stare vacantly at the ground. And wait.

Darkness comes at last. Night birds call. Faraway cattle low mournfully and then are silent.

The next day, no food, no water, and a soldier stands guard to make sure the other prisoners don't share anything with the boys. Frantic with thirst and nearly fainting with hunger, Obulejo is almost relieved when the last morsel and sip have disappeared, and he is no longer taunted with the hope of food or drink.

At regular intervals, different prisoners are led away by a scowling guard. Those left behind hear screams of agony, ending only when the suffering ones are dragged back, half-crippled, and flung to the ground and new victims are selected.

Obulejo averts his eyes from the wounded faces, the bloodied limbs of the tortured. Soon it will be the cane on his bare back, across his calves, over his bowed head.

When his turn comes, it begins with questions he's already heard.

'Will you join the Liberation Army?'

Silence.

Kick.

'You are a traitor.'

'No.'

'You are an infiltrator. Admit it!'

Silence.

Slash.

'Then why do you refuse to join the fight to free our country from the Arabs?'

Silence.

Obulejo is accused of being unpatriotic, decadent, selfish and corrupt.

Again and again the demand is put to him, 'Will you join the fight to free our country – yes or no?'

Silence.

If he says no, the soldiers will beat him or even shoot him. If he says yes, he will be thrown into the fighting and forced to become a killer himself.

His silence enrages his interrogator, who rains down further blows on Obulejo's shoulders, all the while spitting out insults.

'Mangy dog!'

'Useless filth!'

'Less than nothing!'

'Speak, or you will die!'

Silence. Punctuated only by the thud of boots into flesh and the groans that escape from Obulejo's lips. When at last the session is over, Obulejo is dragged back, semi-conscious, and hurled in among the other prisoners.

Each interrogation session brings some unthinkable new horror: sharp metal pincers to squeeze the skin of his thighs and genitals, strokes beyond counting from the mercilessly wielded canes, a burning brand pressed on his skin. Each takes Obulejo to the brink of endurance and beyond, engulfs him in a red haze of suffering. His cries rise like those of a crazed animal, tormented beyond bearing by cruel hunters.

He begs them to kill him now. Longs for his own death.

But his body is not so easily defeated. When he faints, water is dashed in his face, an army boot applied to his ribs.

As the sessions continue, Obulejo slips into such a high wide red terrible wilderness of agony that he cannot even speak to his friends when he is returned to the lock-up.

The youngest and smallest of the prisoners, he has surely borne all he is capable of bearing. Yet, there is no escape. For, cruel as this landscape of agony is, it is far worse to be returned to his full senses and discover that he is still living, forced once again to inhabit his broken and battered body.

11

THREE MORE days pass.

With each beating inflicted by the Rebels, Obulejo withdraws even further from life. His breath becomes shallower and more rapid; he can feel his pulse trembling in his throat. Ochan and Loding whisper encouragement, but Obulejo is unable to respond.

The next day, Akere and Ayella do not return from their interrogation session. No one dares ask what has become of them. They might have given in and agreed to join the Rebels, Ochan whispers. But where are they? Everyone fears the worst.

Older, more hardened prisoners at last begin to mutter among themselves.

'They're just boys,' Obulejo hears one prisoner whisper to the man beside him. 'And that little Ma'di lad isn't even full-grown. Look how small he is. It's not right to beat him so.'

Trucks are coming soon to take them to another barracks, they are told, and until then all prisoners will be put to work cutting poles. In return for their labour they are given a little extra food and water, so they don't become too weak to work.

Obulejo and his companions are marched out with the rest. Obulejo tries to cut poles as directed. Takes a sip of water when prodded, eats a mouthful of cooked maize when the pot is placed on the ground beside the prisoners, washes desultorily when marched to the stream near the camp, but he has become an automaton, barely able to move or speak of his own volition. Existing in a haze of pain.

On day five of their imprisonment, they hear the other prisoners, most of whom are Dinkas, whispering to each other that the following day a truck will come to take all of them away for military service.

'There's a tiny chance we could escape before the trucks get here,' Ochan whispers to Obulejo.

Obulejo does not respond. Curled up on the ground, he listens, eyes shut.

'Some of the Dinkas here were captured after running away from the army,' Ochan says, then adds, 'You know Deng?'

He touches Obulejo's shoulder and gestures towards a tall, brawny man lounging with a group of other Dinka prisoners to one side.

Obulejo nods wearily.

'He's been a soldier since childhood. The Rebel troops are the only family he has known. Even so, he is sickened by what the Rebels have made him do, so he has decided to run to Kenya. He told me he'd help us get away.'

A Dinka is willing to help a Ma'di and an Acholi? Obulejo thinks hazily.

'He said to me, "Tell that little one not to give up, for soon he will be free. Deng will see to it."'

Ochan tells Obulejo Deng's plan. Part of it depends on an older guard who also has agreed to help. He'll turn a blind eye when Deng and the boys slip away.

'Please God it will rain heavily tomorrow,' Ochan says. 'We need rain for the plan to succeed.'

Next day, their prayers are answered. The rain pours down in a never-ending torrent, turning the barracks and its surrounds into a sea of mud. The prisoners are confined to their enclosure.

At nightfall they are called to eat. Obulejo, Ochan and Loding limp out with the rest to where their food is placed on the ground. The teeming rain quickly turns the maize porridge into a thin, watery gruel. Guards and prisoners gobble their rations as quickly as they can, the guards under a thatched roof and the prisoners out in the open.

Obulejo's insides crawl with anxiety.

Everything goes according to plan. Deng asks permission for the boys to collect water to clean off all the mud. He takes them to the fast-running stream a short way from the camp. The guard does not follow. The banks are sticky with red mud, the stream swollen with rushing water and the scrub beyond wild and wet and dark.

Every muscle quivering tensely, Obulejo readies himself.

When they reach the shadowed dip of the bank, the signal comes from Deng.

'Now! Follow me!'

How they run! As silently as they can, they race along the bank, slithering through the bushes, wet prickly branches thwacking their faces in the dark, slick slurrying soil clutching at their feet as they slip and slide, close to the roaring stream.

Panting furiously, Obulejo runs after the others, blindly following their Dinka liberator.

The biggest hurdle now facing the boys is the flooded stream.

Below them, the waters roar and thunder; there is no chance of crossing here. They head downstream where the river is broader and the flow less chaotic. Obulejo has no idea which direction they are heading in. Everything depends on Deng guiding them to the Kenyan border.

Can a Dinka be trusted? he wonders as he runs. It was the Dinkas who created the war and it is their leader who heads the Rebel forces. The Dinkas are so different from the Ma'di; they drink blood and milk from their cattle, and they are warriors who fight first and ask questions later. They think the Ma'di and Acholi are traitors for not joining the Rebel forces. So why would a Dinka rescue three Ma'di and Acholi strangers?

At last they find a place where it seems possible to ford the swirling waters. Obulejo shudders when he sees the black depths. *This would be the time to be a long-legged Dinka,* he thinks, *or a giraffe. Too bad I'm just a Ma'di boy, and will never grow so tall.*

As they step into the flood, Deng takes Obulejo's hand. Obulejo reaches out for Ochan's hand, and Ochan clutches Loding's, and together they let themselves down into the murky water. The force of the current is shocking, beyond the strength of a hundred boys. It drags at their ankles, forcing them downstream. Obulejo's whole body clenches with the effort to stay upright and hold on to the others.

Little by little they make headway through the flood. There is one heart-stopping moment when Ochan stumbles and is swept off balance. The chain of boys sags, the link is broken and all is lost – until Obulejo's flailing hand finds Ochan's and clutches it hard. But where is Deng? In the dark Obulejo can see nothing. Has the river snatched him away?

Finally they stumble out onto the opposite bank, soaked through, coughing and spitting water, shaking and shivering. They fall to their knees, panting but triumphant.

They've made it!

And there is Deng, dragging himself out onto the bank a little way downstream. And although the night into which the four escapees have been liberated is cold and dark, to Obulejo the darkness suddenly seems less smothering, the storm less wild, the way they still have to travel not so hopeless and long. They are free and Deng knows the way to the border. Truly they are blessed to have the Dinka man with them.

Baba would be proud of this man, Obulejo realises suddenly.

Moini has always taught the children, even the tiniest, that they must never let differences between themselves and others rule their lives. For even enemies may turn out to be friends. If you allow them to be.

And Baba is right, as usual.

The storm proves to be both a blessing and a curse, as they push on that night.

The blinding rain and thick dark impede their progress but also wrap them in a cloak of invisibility. They dare not stop, though, in case their absence has been discovered and the soldiers are already out in pursuit.

As Deng scouts for the best and safest route, far from the main road and official checkpoints, Obulejo's spirits rise. Freedom is surely near!

Each time one of the others suggests they rest and take cover, Obulejo argues against it.

'We must hurry,' he urges, 'and get there before the soldiers catch us.'

Obulejo feels that his body is travelling separately from his soul. He feels no pain or cold. He is fired by a single burning desire to keep pushing onwards. Energy rushes through his chilled body. His legs throb, his overstretched muscles jag and cramp, but he pays them no heed.

'Let's go, let's go,' he gasps, over and over.

'How much further to the border?' Ochan asks Deng, at long last, when they seem to have been dragging through the sticky mud forever.

'We're close now,' Deng replies. 'But the guards at the checkpoints search all the convoys and everyone coming through.'

'Then how can we get through?' Loding asks.

'We'll keep going till we find a part of the border that's unguarded,' Deng says. 'They can't post guards along the whole nine hundred miles.'

He leads the boys far away from roads, through a wide sweep of claypan and thornbush and prickly acacias. Here there are no dwellings, no campfires, no soldiers: their footsteps will not be heard.

Everything is hushed, the usual night sounds smothered by the drumming of rain.

Their luck holds.

When dawn breaks Deng announces that they are now on the Kenyan side of the border.

Obulejo is worried that Deng has tricked them. 'We saw no barrier,' he says doubtfully. 'And the land looks just the same.'

'What is there to show we've left one country and entered another?' Loding asks.

Ochan says nothing but he is looking worried too.

Deng laughs. 'Did you think there would be a fence you could follow the whole way to Somalia, or a sign saying *You are now leaving Sudan and entering Kenya*? I tell you, we have crossed the border. But our troubles are not over,' he reminds them. 'We have no rights and no legal status in this new country.'

Their jubilation fades.

'We are truly displaced persons now,' Ochan says.

'With no home and no country,' Loding adds.

But they are still probably better off than poor Akere and Ayella, Obulejo thinks.

'What do we do now?'

'We must go to Lokichogio,' Deng says, 'and report our arrival. The UNHCR will interview us and consider our cases. But first we must clean up.'

Obulejo suddenly realises that he is filthy and bleeding; his clothes are torn and muddy. The others are the same.

They search until they find a borehole. Then each takes a turn pumping the water up for the next, so they can wash. Runnels of mud flow down and puddle at their feet. The cool water feels icy on their chilled bodies. But they are glad to rinse the muck out of their hair, to sluice their limbs and torsos and scrub away at their stained clothes.

Finally they are clean. They wring out their dripping shorts and shirts as tightly as they can. There is no choice but to don the tattered wet garments again. Obulejo feels sick with the cold. And sick with shame. What would his family think if they could see him looking no better than a half naked wild man?

Obulejo spots what looks like a muswak tree, plucks a twig from the branch and hopes fervently that this Kenyan tree does not prove to be poisonous. But soon the familiar foamy, slightly soapy taste fills his mouth and he chews on the twig and scrubs his teeth till his mouth feels fresh and clean.

Shivering and nervous, they set out for Lokichogio.

'UNHCR reception centre for displaced persons?' they enquire of people they meet.

Some throw the ragged group looks of disdain. Others turn away at the sound of Arabic, ignoring their query. Conscious of their dishevelled appearance, the boys and Deng speak quietly and respectfully, repeating their request in Dinka, Acholi, Ma'di and rudimentary English.

Finally they are directed to the right place.

They approach hesitantly, uncertain what to do next.

A tall, skinny Kenyan saunters over to them, and waves imperiously to a big open area in front of a demountable building. The yard is filled with people, variously sitting, standing, lying on bundles or squatting on the ground. All look weary and depressed. A few babies cry fretfully.

'Wait here until you are called,' the official tells them in Swahili. 'Once your name is written down you will be taken to the reception centre for Kakuma refugee camp.'

The day drags on. The sun climbs higher in the sky.

People are called into the office, one at a time or in small groups. Vehicles drive in and out of the compound. Kenyans bustle about, or lie in the shade of the few stunted flame trees. Vultures in the twisted branches look down on the scene with lazy, knowing gazes.

Deng and the boys sit and wait.

They have done all they can. It is up to others now to help them take the next step.

12

THE BOYS DISCUSS whether to give false names when their turn comes to be interviewed.

'It might be safer,' Deng says, 'especially if the soldiers are on our tracks.'

'But it also might reduce the chances of locating our families, or of our families finding out where we are,' Ochan points out.

Obulejo agrees. He is not going to lie. He wants to claim his name; admit to being Obulejo, son of Moini. Trouble tomorrow. Well, the trouble has come. What more can tomorrow bring?

At last they are called, one by one. Obulejo neatly writes the name of his town and district on the proffered form.

'Ma'di?'

'Yes, sir.'

A barrage of questions about how he came to be in Kenya follows, and when he has answered he is waved out to join the others.

There is another wait of several hours. Finally, along with a crowd of other people, they are ushered out to a UN truck. Everyone climbs up onto the tray behind the driver's cab, the young and nimble reaching down to help the old and infirm. Babies and small children are passed over people's heads.

After another delay, a squat man, face shiny with sweat, waddles over and hands a folder of notes up through the window to an official beside the driver.

Finally, just before the sun hits the horizon and dusk falls, the truck roars into life.

They are on their way.

As they bounce along the pot-holed dusty road, Obulejo stares into the deepening shadows. His thoughts tumble about with the jolting truck's rhythm. Kenya. Refuge. Foreign country. Not home. Smells odd. New country. New life. Refugee.

He starts to count his losses. Son of a respected man, member of a large and loving family, hard-working student, destined for college or university and a good job. Now a displaced person. A ragged boy, hunted and hounded, imprisoned and beaten. The winds of war have blown away everything familiar. Scattered his family. Snatched him from the life he knew. What lies ahead? Will he be safe?

When the truck finally grinds to a halt among a maze of buildings, the first thing that meets Obulejo's eye is a blue and white logo – a pair of large hands cupping the silhouette of a very small person. That's how he feels. Shrunken and insubstantial.

The security guards at Kakuma are irritable and impatient. They herd the passengers towards a big building. Obulejo's heart skips a beat. What if the UNHCR officials don't believe him? Accuse him of deserting his country and his people? Decide to send him back?

The wide verandah and the forecourt are crowded with new arrivals. Some slouch or squat in attitudes of resigned patience. A few pace agitatedly, voicing their impatience and frustration in shrill tones. Staff members hustle in and out. A few of the staff are white. Their flushed pink faces stand out among the black ones.

People are ushered inside in groups of three and four.

Finally, as darkness sets in, an official comes out and tells those still waiting that there will be no more interviews that day. People may sleep in the huge marquee behind the building and the office will open at seven-thirty the next morning.

Next day, it is several hours before Obulejo and his friends are called. Inside the building they are left in a passage with closed doors. More waiting. They stand in the corridor with other strangers. There are no chairs. Phones ring. Fans stir the hot air. Flies buzz.

When Obulejo is summoned into an office he stands by the door in silence, again waiting. The woman behind the desk is busy with a sheaf of papers. When she has finished reading, she looks up and fixes her eyes on him. An almost inaudible sigh escapes her lips. She looks hot and tired.

Speaking loudly and clearly, she asks him in English to confirm his name, approximate age, country of origin and whether he is on his own or accompanied by family members. When Obulejo hesitates, she repeats the questions in Swahili.

Obulejo replies in a low voice that he understands and speaks English. He tells his story, eyes downcast and hands clenched behind his back. The woman listens quietly. She does not speak. Perhaps she does not believe him. Perhaps she thinks he has deserted his country for no good reason.

He points to the scars and wounds on his legs. Tears wash his cheeks.

The woman nods. He falls silent. His fate is in this woman's hands. There is nothing more he can do now but wait.

She gives no indication of what she has decided, just hands him a single sheet of paper and tells him to give it to the staff member in the front office by the main entrance. Then she scribbles something in her files and indicates with a wave of her hand that the interview is over.

A woman in a tiny booth by the door takes the paper from Obulejo's outstretched hand and tells him brusquely, 'Wait outside.'

Obulejo pushes open the door and steps out into the blinding heat. He searches the crowd for his companions. He can see no familiar Dinka face towering over the rest of the crowd. *Deng might still be inside*, he thinks. Ochan is nowhere to be seen, either. Perhaps he is still being processed, or he and Deng might already have been sent on to the camp.

Once again Obulejo's friends are being torn away from him.

At last he spots Loding, squatting, head in hands, on the edge of the waiting crowd. The day before yesterday he and Loding were comrades, fiercely united in their desire to escape from the Rebels, holding each other up against the roiling river waters. Brothers for each other. Yet now they are just boys from different tribes – Ma'di and Acholi – with different stories to tell the UNHCR officials.

Obulejo makes no move to approach Loding. *We no longer stand together as family*, he thinks. *In front of these officials we are separate and alone.*

The day drags on. More people enter and leave the reception centre. A drum of water is unloaded from a truck and set up in a corner of the yard. Thirsty people surge towards it.

Pushing through the throng, Obulejo suddenly spots a familiar figure.

'Ochan, my friend,' he shouts.

Ochan turns, with a big grin on his face.

Together they scramble through the jostling crowd till they each get hold of a cup of water.

'Have you seen Deng?' Ochan says as they fight their way back out.

Obulejo shakes his head.

'Loding was among the last to be processed,' Ochan tells Obulejo. 'I saw him in the corridor when I was leaving. He must be here somewhere.'

Obulejo's face grows hot with shame. He has not spared the other boy a thought for hours. Just then, Ochan points to a wildly waving hand. It's Loding, grinning like a monkey! Obulejo and Ochan grin and wave back as Loding pushes his way through the crowd to reach them.

Not long afterwards, a sudden hush falls. Everyone is looking towards one end of the verandah where a UN official now stands, a clipboard and sheaf of papers in her hand. Names are read out. Obulejo's, Ochan's and Loding's are among them. Obulejo is sweating with relief. He clasps Ochan's and Loding's hands.

'We're in,' he says.

'Truly, we are,' Ochan grins.

The boys wring each other's hands.

'Saved!' Loding shouts exuberantly.

'But what about Deng?' Obulejo says. 'His name was not called.'

The boys look at one another.

'Deng must have been refused,' Obulejo says.

'That's not fair,' Loding protests.

'We don't know the full story yet,' Ochan reminds them, 'so for now let us just be grateful that we have been granted residence in Kakuma.'

A bitter prize is theirs – exile from their own country. More bitter, though, is the fate of those who are denied it. Obulejo listens to the angry cries from around the forecourt. People whose claims have been judged false or unfounded are being sent back, to certain death, they shout angrily. Scuffles break out. Security guards appear and hustle the protesting groups away. Obulejo looks on, numb with shock, relieved that he is not among the doomed group, but thinking wistfully that at least they are going home.

In due course he and Ochan and Loding and other successful applicants are taken to the holding centre in the main camp, half a mile away. As he gets nearer, Obulejo glimpses a bewildering array of tents and makeshift shelters built of grass and nylon and coconut palm leaves.

Native people – the Turkana – cross the road in front of the UN trucks with their cattle, and thread their way among the dwellings. They are bare-chested, half naked. The men carry sticks or rifles. Obulejo has never before seen such people. The women have long, beaded earrings and an immense number of strings of beads around their necks. Their skin is oiled and ochred and their shiny breasts are streaked with red dust. Tribesmen carry five-litre jerrycans, which they pause to drink from, before moving on.

At the camp, Obulejo stares about him. Everywhere are crowds of people; black, brown, lighter- and darker-skinned, tall, short, fat, thin, muscly, puny, handsome, ugly. A cacophony of languages, many of which he has never heard before, assaults his ears. A thousand conversations happening all at once, some shouted, as if in rage or argument, others in softer tones. His head begins to spin. He wonders how he will be able to make his way in such a throng. Where will he sleep? How will he live?

His eyes ache from squinting into the sun; his nostrils are choked with dust. There is no familiar, soft, cool grass underfoot, just this endless, gritty, dry earth and a biting hot wind blowing clouds of dust. Red dust coats everything.

They are to remain in the holding camp until a place can be found for them in the main camp, the boys learn. No one is sure when this will be.

Ochan finds out from a Kuku man that Deng has been taken to one of the Dinka areas housing former boy soldiers, and hurries to tell Obulejo and Loding the news. Obulejo is relieved that their rescuer has not been turned away.

The camp is a bewildering and dispiriting place. Buildings and flimsy shelters are jammed together in a parched landscape with scarcely a bush or a tree or a blade of grass to be seen. Dust pools in eddies over the boys' feet. Endless flies land in the corners of their eyes. A lean, hungry-looking dog slinks past and yelps half-heartedly as a missile hurled by a small boy thuds into its loose flank.

Worse, Obulejo senses a constant simmering threat of violence. He glances apprehensively at one hostile, sullen face after another. Whenever a vehicle pulls up and UNHCR workers step down from it, people clamour from all directions, hurling requests and demands.

Inside the holding centre, more questions are asked of the boys, more paperwork is completed, further arguments and discussions take place. They wait and wait. Some people are moved on. Obulejo wonders where a place will be found for them in this makeshift community of the displaced.

He sees himself as the UNHCR workers must see him, just a number, just another refugee among the thousands crammed into the camp, needing to be documented, housed, fed and moved about. No longer is he Obulejo, a Ma'di with a name and a family and a proud tradition. He is just a boy, any boy, without a country to belong to, a home he can call his own.

13

ONE MORNING THREE weeks later a UNHCR official – a grey-haired Kenyan in a rumpled shirt and creased trousers enters the holding centre carrying a clipboard.

'Perhaps today it will be our turn,' Obulejo says.

'Let's hope so,' the others chorus.

Everyone gathers around the official. He gestures for them to sit down. There is a bit of shuffling and jostling, but finally people are ready to listen.

The man speaks in portentous tones, first in Swahili, and then in stilted English.

'One hundred and seventy thousand people, Kakuma camp holds. It divides itself into five zones. Each zone divides into groups. You must go to the place you are assigned. Remain there. No exceptions.'

He pauses, looks around. The onlookers wait patiently.

'Zone one is for Equatorians.'

Loding nudges Obulejo. 'That's us.'

The man goes on. 'Each group divides into smaller groups – five or six people in each.'

Some start to mutter, but the Kenyan waves them to silence and continues to explain.

'Each group, one place, one shelter. Materials for building shelter supplied.'

Obulejo hopes he and Ochan and Loding will be able to stay together, and is relieved when he and his friends are assigned to group 10D. Two others, Acholi boys Okec and Ulum, are to share a shelter with them.

The boys are escorted to a tiny area of bare, dusty ground, and issued with blue nylon sheets stamped with the UN logo, a roll of strong twine and some poles. They must construct a shelter for themselves from these materials. Later they will be given palm leaves to place on the roof, for shade, they are told. They also receive ration cards, a small quantity of beans, oil and maize flour, a few cooking utensils and a bowl, cup and spoon each.

There are so many things to do to secure their survival that Obulejo feels overwhelmed.

'Setting up the shelter is the first and most important task,' Ochan says.

'And fetching water,' Ulum adds.

'But we will manage if we work together,' says Ochan.

'Queuing for rations, too,' Loding says. 'I'm told that can take all day.'

'But if we put our rations together they'll last longer,' Ochan says.

The others nod agreement.

'And take turns to cook,' Okec says.

Ulum laughs. 'We will need strong stomachs then, my brother, when it is your turn, for you have always had five sisters to cook for you and I doubt you can tell the difference between maize and sand.'

Everybody chortles.

'Hunger must spice our food, then,' Ochan says. 'Whether it be *seri* or sand.'

'And we must guard our supplies carefully,' Ulum says.

They have already heard the stories of theft and intimidation around the camp.

'It won't be easy,' Ulum says.

'But it is the best way,' Ochan says.

And so it is settled. They will hold all things in common and take turns at getting water and food, cooking their daily meal and guarding the shelter.

Already the day is hot, so Okec and Ochan go with empty jerrycans to join the queue for water while the others start building the shelter. Neighbours approach Obulejo; they are Ma'di but from different clans. They warn Obulejo and the Acholi boys never to walk about alone.

'Always go in a group or at least in pairs,' they say. 'Nowhere is truly safe, and as newcomers you boys are sure to be targeted.'

At night, when the armed UNHCR security guards have left and the Kenyan troops are back in barracks, they are told, marauding gangs roam the camp, robbing and beating whoever they can find, sometimes shooting and killing their victims. The darkness will not bring rest, but further danger. The boys must take turns keeping watch.

That night, Obulejo hears the sound of guns in his dreams, as he has for many nights now. His legs twitch and pedal all night as though he is still running from the guns, or struggling through dense bush. He is not the only one. Everyone suffers from nightmares: he hears people scream and cry out in their sleep.

He wakes exhausted and depressed.

Daytime is no better. The camp seems to be at the mercy of the armed Turkana herdsmen who roam through unchecked with their donkeys and camels, demanding food from the refugees, though the inmates have little enough for themselves. The sight of guns makes Obulejo's skin prickle with dread. He flinches every time he sees a herdsman with a rifle in the camp. He hears people shouting and arguing.

It's not long before he witnesses his first brutal confrontation.

In the food line, a whisper goes round that supplies are running short. People quickly become agitated. They have been standing for hours in the smothering heat and now it seems they are to go hungry. A group of boys starts to jostle its way forward. Tall Dinkas, former boy soldiers, reputed to have no respect for anybody or anything – even guns. People push back, shouting and cursing at the boys. Obulejo becomes increasingly alarmed as the Dinka boys continue to shove their way violently forward until they reach the cattle race that leads to the food-drop depot.

'*Simama!*' the guards shout, as the boys push against the barricades. 'Stop!'

But the boys rush onwards, deaf to the guards' warnings.

'*Simama wewe murafu!*' the guards yell. 'Stop, you tall ones there!'

The empty-eyed boys recklessly defy the commands.

Obulejo sees the guards cock their rifles and watches in horror as the boys rush into a hail of bullets and pitch forward into the dust.

The crowd scatters, screaming. Obulejo races for the shelter of his flimsy dwelling and that night he and his companions go hungry.

The next day, just as he is about to set off for the food queue again, he notices two women entering the laneway, accompanied by a countryman. He sees another man suddenly step out and block their path. This man mutters something to one of the women, and her countryman immediately rushes at him and starts raining blows on his head and shoulders. A couple of bystanders begin to shout abuse and encouragement, then others, hearing the ruckus, rush over and join in. Within minutes a full-scale brawl is in progress. The angry people scream and shout, gouge and kick and tear at each other, and by the time the security guards arrive, a dozen people are lying bleeding in the red dust.

Obulejo looks on, stunned: it's the second melee he has witnessed in less than twenty-four hours. He has seen fights before, but the speed with which the terrible events of yesterday unfolded and the way the argument today escalated into violence astounds him. It doesn't seem to take much to set people off.

His father always taught him to settle disagreements not with his fists, but by talking things out. *Could be difficult in a place like Kakuma*, he thinks. The Ma'di ways might not stand up here. They belong to the old life, which has been swept away. But he must try to keep them, for Baba's sake.

Obulejo and the others soon discover that on ration day, in order to secure a place in the food line, one of them must rise at three a.m. and wait for many hours in the pre-dawn chill and then in the broiling sun before gradually shuffling forward through a cattle race to the distribution point. Sometimes supplies run out and those still in the queue are turned away empty-handed, and must go through the whole weary business again the following day. There are many days when the boys go hungry. Obulejo is desperate. *There must be an easier way*, he thinks.

And there is. In his second month in the camp, Obulejo steals food, for the first time in his life.

The boys' supplies are all but finished; a handful of maize flour and a spoonful of beans is all they have left. They usually allow themselves a single meal a day, which comes nowhere near satisfying their hunger, but even so, their rations have not stretched far enough. Obulejo knows that many others are faring just as badly, but that knowledge does nothing to fill his empty belly.

As he scuffs along disconsolately in the gathering heat of the morning, he sniffs the enticing aroma of beans cooking. It seems to be coming from a rickety shelter at the end of the lane. When he reaches the shelter, he pauses and listens carefully. There's no sound of people inside and the smell of the beans is making his mouth water. The flimsy door to the shelter is held shut by a piece of twine. Obulejo glances over his shoulder. No one is looking, so he slips the twine off in a single movement and reaches inside. His fingers meet the edge of a large bowl, and then the soft texture of bean stew. He grabs a handful and gobbles it down. It tastes wonderful! He expects to feel a hand on his shoulder and a shout in his ear, but so far so good. He reaches back inside and this time retrieves a bag of maize meal, which he thrusts under his shirt, pausing only to hitch the door shut again before hurrying away.

It is Obulejo's turn to cook that day, and although the others look surprised when a full bowl is set down before them, they say nothing. Perhaps, like him, they are just glad of the warm, soothing fullness in their stomachs.

Daylight fades quickly and except for Ulum and Okec, who are on guard duty that night, they all ready themselves for sleep. But sleep does not come easily to Obulejo. Today he stepped over a line, he realises. His exploit has provided them with food, but he has broken both the Ma'di law of hospitality and God's law: thou shalt not steal.

He cringes at the thought of Moini's shame and anger if he should learn that his son has become a thief. *But what choice did I have?* Obulejo asks himself. *It was hunger that drove me to steal. Survival is the law that rules this new life and I am only one among many. What else can I do?*

But another voice says to him, *Think about the people you stole from, your fellow Sudanese, they're as hungry and desperate as you; haven't they as much right to survive? And you know from the teachings you were raised with that even as stealing fills your belly, it empties your heart of goodness.*

'*Baba ama ata bua rii* – our Father in heaven,' Obulejo mutters. 'Forgive me.'

The food in his belly is a heavy weight now. He tosses and turns on his mat. One thing is certain, however; the shame he feels will not take away the craving for food. Obulejo knows that when the next opportunity arises he will steal again.

Obulejo is both surprised and saddened by how quickly he gets used to the new order of things, and how easy it is to abandon the old laws in the face of continuing hunger. He becomes bolder as his thieving efforts reward his household with extra meals. He feels a swell of pride that he is helping provide for the others in his shelter.

Some of the refugees have set up makeshift stalls and trading posts in the camp. They are the lucky ones, the boys tell each other enviously. Perhaps their families send them money so they can buy goods from their fellow inmates, or goats and chickens from the Turkana and Kenyans. Obulejo wishes he had money to buy meat and bread. No one leaves precious things like that unguarded.

One day, when Obulejo and Ochan are waiting in the line for water, Ochan tells his friend that he too has taken to stealing. Obulejo is surprised at the admission. There is an unspoken rule that if nobody sees you, then you say nothing.

'And I wish one day to become a priest,' Ochan says, hanging his head.

'You stole to help your brothers,' Obulejo reassures him, glancing around to see if anyone is listening to their conversation. 'Do not speak of it any further.'

But it seems Ochan's urge to confess is too strong.

'The first thing I stole was a saucepan,' he says. 'It was outside a shelter. It had been left out to dry, so I grabbed it and took it to one of the traders. "I don't have salt in my house, so I cannot cook," I told the trader, "so I wish to sell my saucepan." Then I took the money and bought meat.'

Obulejo nods. He remembers with pleasure how well they ate that particular day, but he also knows how hard it is for Ochan to throw off the ways they have both been taught to respect and follow.

Ochan lowers his head again. 'My action deprived a mother of the means to cook porridge for her children.'

Obulejo knows just how Ochan feels. 'I never thought I would steal, either,' he says.

But even while he is sympathising with his friend, he decides he'll try out Ochan's method for himself the next time he gets the chance.

He quickly becomes an adept thief. The guilt and the shame are terrible, but the fierce hunger that demands to be assuaged quells the voice of conscience.

At all costs, he must stay alive.

14

ONE ROASTINGLY HOT DAY, Obulejo is standing in line at the rations depot. He arrived early but others had got there even earlier, and all he can look forward to is to stand behind them in line, in the blistering sun, unfed, gasping for water, till he faints from hunger and thirst. He can see that it will take at least two more hours to inch forward to the food distribution point.

He cannot wait a moment longer; he *must* have maize to make porridge with, *now*.

He begins to sidle up the line. He asks a man to let him in, but the man refuses.

The man tells Obulejo, 'This is my place. I have waited since before sunrise. Go back there where you were.'

Go back? Unthinkable. Instead Obulejo moves even further up the line and this time he picks an old woman.

'Please let me in,' he begs her, and the woman starts to make a space for him, but other people in the line shout, 'Get away! This is not your place, get out!'

A red rage engulfs him. He wants to fight those who have denied him a place.

Then, a few paces ahead in the line, someone does just that. Starts a fight. Others soon join in. It doesn't take much to inflame a crowd. The line begins to break up as people scuffle in the dust, their frustrations spilling over into a brawl. The Kenyan guards advance menacingly, Kalashnikovs at the ready, and the crowd scatters. Obulejo sees the attacker rush up the line unnoticed, and follows him. Before people have time to properly reassemble, Obulejo inserts himself forcibly between two weary-looking men. They start to protest but he glares at them and insists, 'No, this is where I was before. You might not have seen properly.'

The two men look at each other tiredly, and Obulejo knows he has won. The men will allow him to go ahead of them rather than create more trouble, for that will bring the guards back again. Today, he will eat when he needs to. Tomorrow he can play the same trick. He can be trouble tomorrow, whenever he chooses.

It's a risky ploy, he knows that. Others have disregarded the warnings of the security guards and paid the price. He remembers the first time he saw troublemakers shot, their bodies jerking to a stop, pitching forward to lie splayed in the dust, bloody and lifeless. It was shocking to witness.

The thing he fears most, though, more than the guns of the guards, is coming face to face with his former captors from the Rebel camp. If he is recognised, Kakuma will offer as little safe refuge as the piles of leaves he once hid under in the jungle. Torture and forced military service will be his fate if he is abducted. His family will never find him then.

Such kidnappings occur daily. Kakuma is less than seventy miles from the Sudanese border, and the Rebel soldiers are allowed free entry to the camp. When the inmates object, the UNHCR staff say, 'But these are your own people,' as if Dinka, Acholi, Ma'di, Moro, Kuku and any other Sudanese tribe are all the same. They make no distinction between those who started the war and those who are fleeing from it. As far as the UNHCR is concerned, they are all just Sudanese.

The Rebel soldiers simply wait till the guards leave at dusk and then snatch people away under cover of darkness. Obulejo has heard the tramping of boots in the night, the muffled screams as people are dragged away, and the sound of gunfire, and has seen people huddled in groups the following day, fearfully discussing the latest raid. And when these incidents are reported to the UNHCR staff, the reply is, 'Are you sure this person you say has been kidnapped was taken against his will? Perhaps he wanted to go home.'

So Obulejo stays hyper-alert, constantly on watch. Whenever he catches sight of a Rebel soldier inside the camp his fists clench and the sour taste of bile fills his mouth. He spends the rest of the day hiding, waiting for the Rebels to depart.

His only respite from fear and hunger comes once or twice a week when he gathers with other churchgoers to sing hymns and listen to the *adungu* players. It's a happy time, almost like being back home. People sing and dance, they smile and chat with each other. On Sunday a Kenyan priest, Father Angelo, conducts the mass. He has been assigned the care of the Christians. He is a kind man, always ready to listen and to advise. He speaks to the young people firmly and gently; tells them not to forget their families, and to put their trust in God. It is only at these gatherings that Obulejo feels he is still the son of his father. Then he is quick to hold a child while a mother rests, or to bring water to the elders, and to listen to their wisdom. He takes heart from Father Angelo's words.

But these times are brief. Most of each day is consumed waiting in line for water or food, skirting violent outbreaks, seeking out opportunities to steal food, and at night Obulejo lies awake for hours listening to people shouting and fighting, or takes his turn to patrol the area around their shelter, to ward off thieves or intruders looking for trouble.

His eyes swim with tears sometimes, when he thinks of the older, more compassionate ways he is losing. But stuck in the camp, with no way out, no magical spell to whisk him away, a boy on his own with no father to defend and guide him and no mothers to feed and nurture him must look after himself.

He must survive as best he can.

An idea slowly begins to take shape in Obulejo's mind. There is one way he might be able to escape the threat of the hated Rebels. He turns the idea over for some time. He knows the others will try to talk him out of it, but he has to do something.

Eventually, he speaks to Father Angelo about his plan. The priest expresses misgivings, but promises to help Obulejo if he can.

'I'm going to leave Kakuma,' he tells the boys in his shelter, one morning.

Six months he has been in this camp. Six months of comradeship, working together as a household and sharing everything, good and bad, but also six months of panic and unceasing nightmares, and six months of becoming a more and more ruthless predator.

'You're crazy,' Ochan says. 'Where will you go?'

'I will apply to go to Dadaab,' Obulejo replies.

The others are shocked. They shout their objections.

'But that is so far away!'

'Nearly to the Somali border.'

'And the Somalis are Muslim. They hate us.'

'What kind of comrade leaves his brothers behind?' Ulum demands.

'You will never get permission to transfer,' Ochan adds. 'You think a refugee can go wherever he wishes? Without papers? Who will give this worthless boy papers?'

'Stay with us,' the others plead. 'Don't leave.'

Obulejo knows they are afraid he will become one of the thousands of nameless and homeless dead.

They don't believe he'll go through with it. Even now his parents may be searching for him, they argue, and if he is nowhere to be found it will break his father's heart. Dadaab is a long way away, close to the town of Garissa. It may be far, far worse than Kakuma. He might even get killed on the way.

'My parents may be dead already,' Obulejo replies, the words striking terror into his heart as he speaks them. 'I must be responsible for myself. And for putting myself out of reach of the Rebels for good,' he adds.

'You will be jumping out of the path of a stampeding elephant into the mouth of a hungry lion,' Ochan says. 'Even if you obtain permission to leave Kakuma, how will you get to Dadaab?'

Obulejo shakes his head silently. The boys in his shelter have become the closest thing to family he has here in Kakuma. He is loath to lose them. But he has to go. He isn't willing to wait around while there's a chance of being taken by the Rebels.

'Many times I have teased you for bearing the name "Trouble tomorrow",' Ochan says, 'but I fear this mad plan will now make it come true.'

They put their many arguments to him all over again, but nothing persuades Obulejo to change his mind.

Finally they give up. 'You will leave Kakuma, whatever we say, we see that now,' they say.

Obulejo nods.

It takes him another six months to gain permission to transfer to Dadaab. Six months!

Six more months struggling to get enough to eat and drink and to stay clear of the Rebels; six more months of heat, hunger, thirst and violence. And six months of struggling with UNHCR forms, interviews and meetings, having his hopes dashed then raised again until at last he gains the necessary documents. It's a tortuous process, and success is only made possible by the efforts of Father Angelo, who takes pity on him and manages to successfully plead Obulejo's case to the camp authorities. The priest also provides his bus fare and a few extra Kenyan shillings.

'Divide the money into separate bundles and keep these in different pockets,' Father Angelo advises. 'You will meet several people, soldiers or officials, who won't let you proceed unless you give them a cash "consideration".'

Then he thrusts a camera and a spare pair of trousers into Obulejo's hands.

'I have little to spare, but these may prove useful in your new life. You can always sell them if you need to. Godspeed, my son.'

Obulejo shakes the priest's hand warmly. *There are still good people in the world*, he thinks. And perhaps, when he has shaken the dust of Kakuma off his feet, he will be able to make a new start, and begin to behave in a way that will give this kind priest and also his parents more reason to respect him.

The bus journey takes two days – long, dusty, tiring, frustrating and heart-stopping days, along winding, broken roads, passing through endless checkpoints manned by security guards with guns.

At several checkpoints the officials stare at Obulejo's papers for several minutes before muttering that 'something seems not to be in order' and this means Obulejo cannot travel on. Then they quietly suggest there is a way to fix the problem. Obulejo hands some money over, thanking God for the priest's gifts and advice.

One guard is more blatant, saying that there will be no proceeding past his checkpoint until money passes hands. Obulejo dares not refuse. He keeps his eyes lowered and calls the man 'sir' and 'baas', but it sticks in his craw, making him smoulder with frustrated rage.

A guard at one checkpoint accuses Obulejo of smuggling. He insists on stripping and searching him. He makes Obulejo wait, naked, in the guard-house almost to the moment the bus is due to depart. Obulejo hears the bus engine grinding into life. If he misses the bus he will be stuck in this guard-house indefinitely, with no friends, no one to help him, no one even knowing where he is or caring why he does not turn up at Dadaab. Just another lost boy in this war.

He considers making a naked dash for it, but realises that even if he reaches the bus, the driver will not let him on.

At last, when all seems lost, the guard hurls the clothes at him. As Obulejo dashes for the bus, running and jumping and hopping as he struggles into his trousers, he hears the guard's mocking laugh behind him.

15

JUST AS THE boys predicted, Obulejo arrives in Dadaab to find himself in an even worse situation.

'We cannot register you as a bona fide refugee,' the UNHCR official says, when Obulejo is taken to his office along with other new arrivals. 'Dadaab is for Somalis. Kakuma was set up for Sudanese boys like yourself. That's the agreement your government made.'

Obulejo keeps his face expressionless but his stomach is roiling and his mind spins in panic. His position is perilous. Without refugee status he will be given no rations. How will he survive?

'So why have you come here?' the UNHCR officer demands.

Obulejo begins to explain but is cut off mid-sentence.

'You should have stayed in Kakuma,' the officer says.

With that, he bends over his papers and begins to scribble furiously. Stricken, Obulejo remains standing before the desk. What can he do now? He has no way of making the return journey on his own, and nowhere else to go.

Finally the officer looks up. He sighs. 'But now you are here I suppose we must find somewhere for you.'

Obulejo is escorted to a section of the camp where the few Sudanese inmates of Dadaab are housed, huddled together. This section is heavily fenced with thick thornbushes banked up against and twined through wire mesh, to protect the refugees from attack by the Somalis, who deeply resent both the presence of the Sudanese and the incursions of the Kenyans into an area they consider to be theirs by right.

The enmity between Christians and Muslims is severe, Obulejo learns, as it is between different races and tribes. The Sudanese sector in Dadaab contains people of many different tribes, some of whom, Obulejo is well aware, have always hated one another back home. But in this foreign land they have been forced to set aside their differences and to look upon themselves as all Sudanese together.

The Ma'dis welcome him as a brother, find him a place to sleep in their crowded quarters and offer him maize porridge, which he accepts gratefully.

They gather round and fling questions at him.

'Why have you come to Dadaab?' an elder asks.

Obulejo explains.

A younger man asks, 'But how did you get permission to leave Kakuma?'

'And how are things there?' another says.

'My family – did you see my family there?' another wants to know. 'My mother or my children? They are called —'

And names are flung at Obulejo from every direction till his head spins. Everyone is hungry for any word of the whereabouts or fate of family members. He tells them what he can.

They quickly fill him in on the difficulties of life in Dadaab: the scarcity of food, of clean drinking water, of coals for their cooking fires or adequate protection against the dreadful sandstorms that sweep through from time to time. And there are constant attacks by their Somali neighbours.

'It is not safe to leave the Sudanese area on your own,' a grizzled elder says. 'Even going about in a group has its dangers. The Somalis shout insults and hurl stones at anyone who steps outside. At night angry people bang on the fences, shouting and firing at random. And you risk being shot if you venture beyond the camp's perimeters.'

What they cannot tell him, he knows, is how to feed himself when he has no ration card. They have pressed on him some maize porridge, but will they continue to do so?

What have I done? Obulejo begins to wonder. *How am I to survive here if I cannot get food and water?*

Like a bird in a snare, he feels the noose of starvation tightening around his neck.

There are no Rebel soldiers here, but, to Obulejo's dismay, in its own way Dadaab is proving to be just as dangerous as Kakuma. On his first night there, looters succeed in breaking down a section of the fence surrounding the Sudanese compound and several shelters are robbed. Seven people are injured; two are killed.

The next day Obulejo witnesses a shooting. Thieves smash in the metal door of a nearby shelter and open fire. A bullet hits one of the occupants. He goes down. Panicked people scatter like the wind.

Is there nowhere without guns and fighting?

It seems not.

At night, boys and men patrol the fence in the Sudanese compound, standing guard against thieves and rioters.

The biggest threat, Obulejo is warned, comes from the *shiftas*, ruthless Somali warlords who strike terror into people's hearts, just as the Rebel soldiers had in Kakuma. The *shiftas* attack and kill with impunity.

And just as in Kakuma, there is never enough water to go round and never enough to eat. Those with ration cards, who get to stand in line, are the lucky ones, no matter how long they have to wait. Obulejo envies them. He is grateful to the Ma'di who share their food with him, but he quickly realises that having one extra person to feed is fast depleting their supplies. They are probably wondering when he will start to contribute to the group, rather then being a drain on their resources. He is not close kin; their own families are having to go short to feed him.

By the start of his second week, Obulejo becomes aware of a change of attitude in his Ma'di hosts: there is now a coolness, verging on hostility. He no longer feels welcome. His suspicions are confirmed when he approaches the shelter one afternoon and hears raised voices from within.

'For how long will we keep supporting him without him giving to us?'

And a second voice: 'Once our food gets finished —'

The voices break off abruptly as he enters, but he knows his days as their guest are coming to an end.

What then? He has no idea.

That evening, before the men go out on patrol, the older Ma'dis call Obulejo to meet with them. There is something they need to discuss, they tell him. His heart sinks. This is it. His marching orders.

'We are all Ma'dis,' the oldest man begins.

'We have all come from far away,' another interjects, 'from different counties.'

'And all of us are in need,' a third adds.

Obulejo glances around the faces in the group. They seem closed, antagonistic. He readies himself for further unwelcome news.

The elder waves the others to be silent. He has more to add. 'We have been supporting you.'

Heads waggle in agreement. *Then why has no one gone to the UNHCR to plead for me?* Obulejo thinks.

'And now it has become too difficult for us to continue supporting you.'

Obulejo receives the news with downcast eyes. He knows what will come next.

'If you can get money,' the elder continues, 'then we can give you dry maize in return. We must have money to pay for the grinding of our maize.'

'We must buy salt and oil as well,' his wife adds. 'If you can help pay for them, we can share food with you as before.'

'But if you cannot contribute,' the elder concludes, 'you will not be able to continue eating with us. That is how it is.'

Obulejo signals dumbly that he has heard and understood. He does not trust himself to speak. Terror clutches his stomach. Why was he so foolish as to come here? At least in Kakuma he was certain of food every day – or almost every day. He knew how everything worked and he was among thousands of his own countrymen, not a mere handful. It's true there are no Rebel soldiers in Dadaab, but he could just as easily be murdered here. How could he have imagined outrunning the danger?

As if to confirm his fear, the evening call to prayer begins to ring out over the camp: '*Allahu Akba* – God, Most Gracious, Most Merciful.'

The call of those who hate us, Obulejo thinks. *There will be no mercy for me.* All night long his thoughts whirl and pitch and swirl, around and around, always reaching the same conclusion.

He is lost.

There is nowhere to turn.

Nothing he can do.

Then his terror turns to blind rage. If John Garang had not started this war, Obulejo would still be at home with his family. It's all the Dinkas' fault. He wishes they would disappear off the face of the earth!

All night the storm in him rages.

Dawn breaks, bleak and hopeless. Then he remembers the morning prayers of his childhood, led by his father, and a hymn they sang together.

Father, our praise and prayers a-scending.
Sing hallelu-jah, hallelu-jah, oh King of Cre-a-a-tion.

Over and over, the words repeat themselves in his aching head, and with them comes a renewed conviction that there must be a way to survive, if only he can find it. He will pray to the Heavenly Father and trust that his prayers will be answered.

As the day begins to get underway, Obulejo approaches the elders. 'I thank you for supporting me,' he tells them. 'But I must go now.'

He observes the relief with which his announcement is met, a relief they try politely to conceal. No one invites him to stay longer, nor is he asked where he will go or how he will live. Numbly, Obulejo gathers his few possessions. As he turns to go, a woman hands him a tiny bundle of maize. He nods his thanks and steps out of the shelter.

He has no idea what to do next.

All that day he trails along rutted laneways, behind groups of Sudanese men, close enough for protection, not so close they will turn on him and chase him away. When darkness falls he huddles against the side of a nylon tent. At least no one rushes out to chase him away.

All night he hears the screams of people being beaten, and of those who cry out in their sleep. He watches the flickering shadows of the men on patrol, as they keep guard.

He makes the small quantity of maize last two days. When he has been without food for a further three days and without sleep for the same number of nights, he realises he will die soon if he does not find a way to get food and a safe place to rest. So he hatches a desperate plan. He singles out a boy as unkempt and starved-looking as himself and approaches him with the plan. The other boy agrees readily.

Together they cruise the laneways, looking for people carrying bags or bundles. Eventually they spot an old man hurrying along with a bulging brown bag clasped to his chest. Instinct tells Obulejo that there is something valuable in that bag. He signals to his accomplice to hang back.

'Hey you!' he shouts at the man. 'We met yesterday and you insulted me!'

The man starts to back away. 'No, it was never me. I have never seen you before.'

'Are you saying I am lying?' Obulejo demands, fiercely. 'It was you, I say!'

He slaps the man. The man slaps him back. In the ensuing fight the man drops the bag. Obulejo's accomplice grabs it and runs off. Other people join the fight. When Obulejo manages to extricate himself and catch up with the boy they triumphantly share their spoils. Bread, and two shirts and also a watch they can probably trade for food.

They rush deeper into the laneways of Dadaab, to a stall far away from the scene of the attack, and buy cups of hot sweet tea and a vegetable curry which they mop up with the stolen bread. Delicious!

'My name is Muloko Lorok,' the boy tells Obulejo, as they are eating. 'In Bari it means "bad spirit".'

Obulejo grins, and wonders if Muloko Lorok's parents named him that, or whether the boy has taken the name himself, to give him the courage to fight and steal.

That night Muloko Lorok leads Obulejo to the shelter he shares with nine others. Hunkered down in a tiny space by the door, Obulejo manages to snatch a few hours of fitful sleep.

Next morning the ravenous beast of hunger begins to tear at him once again. He confers with Muloko Lorok and they head towards the market area to trade the shirts for money. They buy a small parcel of grain, and with the watch they head towards a butcher's stall at the periphery of the Somali sector. They crave meat.

The area around the butcher's stall is seething with hungry customers, all shouting to gain the stallholder's attention. At last the boys reach the front of the queue. They hold up the watch, and the Somali nods. He hands them a hunk of meat. Obulejo clutches it tightly as they start to push their way through the crowd. Now they must buy wood with their few remaining shillings, so they can cook the meat. Obulejo savours the prospect of the feast – until the meat is snatched abruptly from his hands. Muloko Lorok sets up such a howl of protest that people rush to see what's happening. Accusations are shouted and denied, then fists begin to fly.

The brawl quickly escalates into a battle, tribe against tribe. More and more people join in. They scream and yell and tear at each other, punching and kicking. Some people fall in the dust and are trampled on; others limp away, blood flowing from their mouths and noses.

Obulejo and Muloko Lorok flee when they see security guards coming to disperse the crowd.

'Aii-eeh,' Muloko Lorok wails, 'our feast is lost.'

Then Obulejo discovers that in the scuffle he lost hold of their parcel of grain.

Muloko Lorok spits into the dust. 'Why didn't you guard it properly?'

Obulejo has no answer.

'That's it, then,' Muloko Lorok says. 'You have no skill as a thief.' He turns on his heel and disappears into the crowd.

Obulejo is flooded with despair. He's had one decent meal, but now the future is as uncertain as ever.

His chances of survival look bleak.

16

'OBULEJO!' SOMEONE IS calling his name.

He spins round, ready to fight, but sees three young Ma'di men beckoning to him. They are going into the bush, they tell him, to collect firewood and look for food. He is welcome to come with them if he wishes.

Limp with relief, Obulejo agrees. He could sell firewood and thus fill his empty belly.

Then his relief turns to doubt.

'Do you have permission to leave the camp?'

The young men laugh uproariously.

'Do *you* have permission to starve?' they counter.

Obulejo hangs his head. He is still the same good law-abiding boy at heart, in spite of the crimes he has perpetrated, and he knows both the UNHCR and the chairman of the Ma'di sector have forbidden people to go beyond the camp's perimeters.

'But it's dangerous out there!' he protests.

The native people collect firewood and bring it on horseback to sell in the camp. They are quick to attack people venturing out to collect wood for themselves. Many have been killed.

The young men show Obulejo the bows and arrows they have concealed in their clothes.

'We can protect you with these,' they tell him.

This assurance and Obulejo's growling stomach decide the matter for him.

As they approach the thornbush perimeter fence, an elder stops them, concern written clearly on his face.

'Where are you boys going?'

The boys cross their legs, mimicking an urgent need to relieve themselves.

'To help ourselves.'

'Airport.'

Obulejo knows that the area surrounding the camp where people go to relieve themselves has been dubbed 'airport' because it is so flat and open. People go in families or groups, to 'help themselves', squatting to gain what little privacy they can, while others stand guard.

The elder nods. 'Be careful. Make sure you stay together.'

Once outside the fence, Obulejo and his new friends search for wood, glancing around them constantly. They also look for edible leaves and roots.

'What about making snares?' Obulejo suggests. 'We might get a bird.'

The others are keen. They search for cow hairs to plait into a loop. In his old life, now a fast-fading dream, Obulejo's skills were considered excellent. His older brothers taught him well. It is time to see if he still has the knack.

He ties the first snare with a small length of nylon thread he has in his pocket. For the next, he uses the cattle hairs. One of the boys offers a few scraps of maize, which Obulejo places inside the loops. From behind a tree, he watches and waits silently, till an unsuspecting wood dove stretches its beak towards the grain. In the blink of an eye it is trapped. Success!

The bird that approaches his second snare is more wary. It snatches the grain and escapes before the snare can do its work. Obulejo reloads the snare and waits an agonisingly long time before catching a second dove.

The boys are jubilant.

'Make sure we save some of our firewood, so we can grill the birds when we get back,' one boy says.

'*If* we make it back,' another of the hunters laughs.

'So far so good,' the third boy adds.

Obulejo's empty stomach almost knocks against his ribs in anticipation of the feast. Memories of the rich smell of the meals the women used to prepare at home come back to tantalise him.

'Next time I'll try and take the bird alive,' he says.

'Yes,' the boys agree, 'then we can sell it to buy bread or some sugar for hot tea.'

They have to search far and wide to make up their bundles of wood. Most of the twigs and branches closer in have already been scavenged.

'The longer we stay out and the further we go, the greater the risk,' the boys tell Obulejo, 'but it is worth it.'

Late in the afternoon they straggle back to camp dusty and tired, each with a bundle of sticks and knobby branches on their shoulders. Eagerly they discuss what they might purchase with the money they will get. Beans, they decide unanimously, as a change from maize porridge, plus oil and salt of course, and if they are lucky, tea leaves and perhaps even a spoonful of sugar. And there is still the prospect of those delicious birds.

Obulejo walks back with the other boys, glad he has proved himself among them, grateful that he will soon have something in his stomach.

Night is falling as the boys suck every last morsel of juice from their fingers, savouring their feast, longing for more.

Now the problem of where to spend the night raises its head again. Obulejo pictures another night spent cringing in the shadows while Somali warlords and their henchmen rampage through the camp, beating and killing anybody they find. Will he never be safe?

He is so absorbed in his forebodings he does not notice the looks that pass between the boys.

'You come with us,' one says abruptly.

Obulejo is startled. 'I don't understand.'

'Tonight you come to our shelter,' the boy repeats.

Such relief! Obulejo quickly accepts.

He follows the boys back to their shelter, and eases his body down into the sliver of space he has been allocated. There is just room to stretch his legs out, but he must keep his arms folded across his chest so as not to jab those sleeping either side of him. Despite the discomfort, the presence of others wedged close lulls him to sleep.

Deep in the night a blood-curdling scream hurls him awake. He hears the sound of running feet, coming closer, then thankfully retreating, followed by the measured footsteps of their guard pacing to and fro outside the shelter.

That is the end of sleep for Obulejo. He spends the next few hours trying to decide whether he dare approach the

UNHCR office again, to plead his case. Back and forth the argument in his head goes.

But getting food is more urgent. In the morning he must leave the camp again, hunt more birds, gather firewood and whatever else he can find. What else is he to do? Continue to attack unwary people and rob other shelters? Or, as a final resort, throw himself in front of the guards' rifles, like those boy soldiers in Kakuma? Then at least his troubles would be at an end.

For a few moments he savours the prospect – no more struggling. But what if his parents found out? How could they bear the shame of their son's cowardice? No, he must struggle to stay alive at all costs. For his family's sake. And to show the Dinka that a Ma'di boy can be equal in strength and courage to the most ferocious of the Rebels. He grinds his teeth, wishing a Dinka would appear before him right now: if only he had a sharp-bladed panga in his hand, what wouldn't he show those war-crazy people!

His fantasies grow: he'll not only teach the Dinka a lesson, but also the Somalis who call names and attack the Christians and throw great stones to kill them! All he needs is a panga and a clutch of barbed Ma'di arrows to fire off in a volley and inflict deadly wounds that will fester and poison the blood of his enemies. And as his victims drop to the ground, crying out in agony, he'll finish them off with his panga and count the dead bodies with glee.

And the Ma'dis, his own people, who have refused to continue to shelter and protect him according to Ma'di customary lore, they will be punished too. He pictures himself striding back to camp, a string of doves slung over his shoulder, enough to buy beans and oil and bread and even meat for many – and tea and sugar. The eager imploring glances of those who have turned him out to fend for himself will meet him and he will return them with scorn and disdain. Off he will stride to the markets, command a front position for himself before the Somali butcher's stall, and call out for meat for soup.

Suddenly his fantasy dissolves and he is overcome by shame and bitter despair. Why is he railing against his own people? Did they not feed him when he was starving? It is not their fault they could not continue to do so.

Turning the poison arrows of bitterness against others will kill his Ma'di spirit and make enemies of his own people. No, that isn't the answer.

Exhausted, Obulejo finally drifts back into a restless sleep.

The next day, in the chill of early morning he rises swiftly and stumbles out of the shelter. A wisp of the dream that visited him just before waking lingers for a tantalising second, and with it a sense of familiar presences.

Baba!

The elder brothers.

Mama Natalina and Mama Josephina.

The sisters, aunties and uncles.

Grandfather.

The images falter and dissipate, but in their wake comes an afterglow, a faint aroma of cooking fires, of henna, of the rich, warm smell of his father's skin, the good damp soil of gardens and of green and growing things, and the sounds of singing, feasting and dancing. Home. Perhaps he is hallucinating.

He doesn't care. It's just so wonderful to see them all again, even in a dream.

None of the boys in the shelter is stirring. Obulejo is grateful for this quiet moment alone with his family. He savours it for a few moments then sets out to find water to wash with. He cannot bear to be dusty and dishevelled a moment longer. Perhaps it's the brief glimpse of his mothers, the memory of the steadying presence of his father and the companionship and protective camaraderie of his older brothers that have challenged him to take heart and try again – and not to despair.

This afternoon he will go to the open-air church service and sing hymns with the other Christians and afterwards join in the dancing and lose his troubles for a while. Try to think of those among whom he lives as brothers, not enemies. Open himself to another way.

It takes him almost till noon to get hold of a small quantity of brackish water, in return for carrying heavy jerrycans for a number of people. Careful not to waste a drop, he rinses the dust from his hair and face and swabs his arms and legs and body.

When he has finished washing, he tears a wide strip from the bottom of each leg of his trousers, and rolls the cloth into a bundle. *I will sell this for a handful of maize, or whatever I can get for it*, he determines. Then what? He pushes the thought away. *Just get through today*, he tells himself.

As he walks back through the Sudanese sector of the camp, keeping close to fellow countrymen for safety, he ponders his situation. There are some things he cannot change. He cannot go home. Cannot find his family, except in dreams and visions. Cannot continue his interrupted schooling. He must stay here in the camp until the chance to make a new life comes. And while he is here, his first needs are food, shelter and water.

The choices are clear. He can continue risking capture by sneaking into the bush for firewood, birds and other game, but there is no certainty that he will not come back to camp empty-handed, if he makes it back at all. He can become a predator, looting and stealing and matching violence with violence. Or he can find some other solution.

The stakes are high. His future may depend on what he decides today.

He has watched his parents and older brothers work tirelessly to improve the family's fortunes. They have served God and always shown compassion and courtesy to others. He ponders the example of his elders and the notions of work and service and right action.

Finally a solution presents itself. Why doesn't he try to set up a small business? He should have thought of this before. For the time being he will continue the dangerous practice of going into the bush to collect firewood to sell in the camp but also he can offer small services in return for food or water or a few shillings, as he had this morning – fetching and carrying for others, standing in the line to get water for them, queuing at the butcher's, doing whatever people require.

His step quickens. There might be hope, after all, and he may be able to take his place with pride as a Ma'di once again.

Eager now to greet his countrymen, to pray with them under the scanty shade of the tree they have chosen to mark their place of worship, and then to lose himself in the singing and dancing, Obulejo hurries towards the square.

17

DUST RISES IN the shimmering heat of early afternoon. Feet stamp and shuffle as the dancers pick up the beat of the music. Obulejo joins in eagerly. Like most Sudanese, he has always loved to sing and dance, to feel the music take hold of him and fill his being. When he sings, when he dances, he is in his right place.

The *adungu* players are tireless and the dancing goes on for a long time. The harsh desert air rings with the sound of songs shouted rapturously and the dusty earth echoes the beat of stamping feet.

Afterwards, panting and sweating, people shake hands, grateful for being together in celebration. Obulejo passes from person to person, greeting each member of the makeshift congregation.

Suddenly he hears his name called. He turns and squints into the blinding sunshine. Who is summoning him? The voice is familiar. So is the tall figure approaching: a loping gait he knows well.

His face splits into a wide grin and he holds out his hand in greeting. 'Maku!'

'Obulejo!'

The two shake hands cordially.

'It is so good to see you, my friend,' Maku says.

'You too,' Obulejo replies. 'But how did you come to be here?'

Maku describes the arduous route from his seminary in the north, through Ethiopia, to northern Kenya and Dadaab.

'And yourself?' Maku says.

Obulejo quickly recounts his journey from Torit, his capture by the Rebels, his escape, then finally arriving in Kakuma, and his fear, given the constant Rebel presence in the camp, of being recognised by them and recaptured. He explains how Father Angelo helped him obtain a transfer to Dadaab.

'I see,' Maku says slowly.

Obulejo hangs his head. 'But they have refused to register me at this camp. Dadaab is not for the Sudanese, they told me.'

Maku nods. 'That's right. The UNHCR has made an agreement with the government of Kenya, and all the Sudanese in Dadaab are being relocated to Kakuma.'

Obulejo considers this information silently. So his foolhardy trip has been for nothing. Before long he will be back where he started.

Obulejo and Maku talk together for over an hour.

'It is so good to be with you, my friend,' Obulejo says, finally, 'but now I must go. I have to sell this cloth so I can buy sugar.'

He points to his small bundle of cut-off trouser legs. 'When I sell that sugar to others, a spoonful at a time, I'll buy grain.'

'Me too,' Maku grins and indicates a pile of firewood by his feet. 'I use this to buy *seri*. I keep a portion of it for myself and sell the rest.'

Obulejo grins back.

'We can be partners if you wish,' Maku says.

Obulejo nods. And it's settled, just like that. He will go into business with Maku. They will sell food.

They'll work hard to collect firewood and hunt birds and sell these to people in the camp who have money. There are various ways of getting money in the camp: some earn it through their own labours, others trade their possessions, and the lucky ones receive gifts of cash from their relatives, through the UNHCR.

They will not be short of customers. Hunger is a constant presence in the life of refugees. And gradually, as they earn more money and build up their stocks, they'll be able to offer a range of foodstuffs for sale. It might not work, but they'll give it a try. And Maku will make a trustworthy business partner, Obulejo knows. Their families have been close friends for years.

When Maku discovers that Obulejo has nowhere to live he invites him to join his own household. Two other Ma'dis share his tent, he tells Obulejo, and there is enough room for a fourth. Obulejo accepts gratefully. He can hardly believe his fortunes have turned, just like that. Yesterday he was looking forward only to starvation and a violent death and now he has gained a good and honest friend and partner and been given a less crowded place to live and a way to support himself – three inestimable gifts. He struggles to find words to express his thanks, but Maku just claps him on the shoulder and says, 'Come, now we must go and sell our wares.'

With the shillings they receive, they purchase tea leaves and sugar. Together they carefully sort the goods into tiny bundles, to offer for sale. A teaspoon of sugar, another of tea leaves. They also buy three packets of cigarettes; these they will sell as single cigarettes or as bundles of two and three, whatever their customers can afford.

While they work, they discuss their plans, and talk about life in the camp.

'Now we are living as brothers – one family,' Maku says, 'we must try to live peacefully together and always respect each other.'

Obulejo nods eagerly, relieved that Maku is taking on the role of older brother.

'You can always share with me any difficulties you are having and I will help you work them out. And remember never to go out alone,' he adds. 'I want my younger brother to stay safe.'

'Thank you, my brother,' Obulejo replies.

'You must take particular care on *Salat Jumu'ah*, the Muslim Friday prayers,' Maku cautions, and for a few sober moments both ponder the discord that exists between Muslims and Christians.

Their conversation then turns back to their new business venture.

Obulejo can hardly wait to get started. Both he and Maku are prepared to work hard. Obulejo is young and strong, Maku older and steadier and more experienced in the ways of Dadaab. They'll make a good team. It will be honest work.

'By helping others, we can help ourselves,' Maku says.

Obulejo savours the prospect like a silver fish, gasping on the bank under a relentless sun, suddenly finding itself back in the embrace of the life-giving waters of the Nile.

Obulejo and Maku set to with a will. For the next three weeks they take the daily risk of going out of the camp to gather firewood and catch birds, then they sell these things and buy food to hawk to fellow inmates. And when they have amassed a small but useful sum of money, they buy wheat flour to begin baking bread.

They use a large, empty oil tin to construct a bread oven, prying one end off and making an opening through which to insert the loaf. Then they set the tin on the ground lengthwise and build a fire on top. It works like a dream. People are eager to buy the bread. Obulejo is kept on the go, gathering wood for the bread oven, preparing the dough and baking the loaves. Even when his brief hours of sleep are interrupted by nightmares or disturbances in the camp he is still keen to get started again early each morning. The work, though physically taxing, soothes him.

And it brings its rewards. After feeding themselves and seeing to their own needs, Maku and Obulejo are able to set aside a few shillings from time to time. Slowly their savings grow. They no longer have to look for work washing or carrying things for other people. They are meeting a strong need in providing relief from the monotonous refugee diet of maize porridge day after endless day.

Obulejo's restless anxiety begins to recede as the rhythm of regular work orders his days, and regular meals help ease his hunger and resentment. Rage flares up in him less violently and less often.

Perhaps the Dinka are not to blame for all his troubles. Perhaps the Somalis are suffering just as he is.

Best of all he can face the other Ma'dis unashamed when he sees them in the laneways or meets them at prayers or in the choir sessions that Maku leads. No longer does he feel separated from his own people by shame.

Obulejo and Maku decide that their next venture will be to set up a café.

'We'll call it the Hotel Bombay,' Maku says. 'I had a friend who travelled to Bombay once. We will name our café in honour of my friend.'

Obulejo agrees happily. Hotel Bombay is a great name.

They count out their savings. Not really enough to get them started. So Obulejo sells his one remaining possession, the camera the priest gave him, and he and Maku pool their money to buy the materials for their café.

They choose a spot on the main pathway among the tangle of makeshift dwellings: people come and go along this lane all day and word of the new café will quickly spread.

The Hotel Bombay is a tent, where customers may eat under cover, protected from burning sun, desert winds and constantly blowing sand. Six poles support a roof of nylon sheeting, which Maku and Obulejo cover with grass. Nylon twine secures the tent walls, and at the entrance they place a painted sign: *HOTEL BOMBAY – WELCOME.*

'Two shillings for bread and a cup of sweet tea,' they tell people passing by. 'And if you can afford it, beans or meat stew with bread.' The special wheat bread Obulejo bakes is popular; people are sick of beans and maize flatbread. They yearn for soft wheat bread and for meat.

Every day the Hotel Bombay is filled with customers who come to rest, to eat, to chat and to sip sweet tea and forget their troubles for a while.

Obulejo and Maku are very pleased with its success.

Life is hard, but cooking and serving lunch together each day and singing and dancing in the afternoons several days each week gives Obulejo a measure of steadiness and order – and provides a small oasis from the violence and despair that surround them.

Sometimes Obulejo is even able to hope that one day the war will be over, this refugee nightmare will end and he will be able to go back home to his family.

18

BUT THERE ARE still days when nothing can lift his spirits. These are the days when sandstorms blot out the landscape and smother the whole camp in grit, or when hours of trying to get hold of some clean water yield no results and Obulejo is forced to buy filthy water from local tribesmen; days when tribal hatreds flare up over trifles and acts of violence disrupt life in the camp for the hundredth or the thousandth time. Then the old fears rise and despair threatens to overwhelm him.

How long will he have to inhabit this overcrowded camp, struggling for food, water, firewood, shelter and living space? Where too many people are crammed together without enough latrines and are forced to foul the surrounding land. Disease is rife.

One morning Obulejo wakes with a fever. His body is on fire, his bones ache and his head throbs. He has a burning thirst. When he tries to get up, he cannot make his arms and legs obey. He falls back on his mat with a moan. The tent is empty, except for him. A beat of fear begins to drum in his head. He has no family in Dadaab. Will he be left alone to die?

Maku returns a few hours later, and approaches cautiously. Obulejo understands his caution. Everyone in Dadaab has a fear of illness. There are few doctors to treat the hordes of sick people.

'What is wrong?' Maku enquires.

Obulejo cannot answer. His tongue is thick and dry. To his dismay his eyes swim with tears he cannot hold back. He cannot tell Maku that it is his mother and brothers and sisters he longs for, Mama Natalina's porridge to build his strength, and Mama Josephina's tender nursing.

For days all he can manage is a few sips of water at a time. When the shivering and the aching finally stop, Obulejo has become so weak he can do nothing more than crawl to the tent door and rest there, gasping at the effort.

Another day passes before he is strong enough to bathe and two more days before he can shakily rejoin Maku at the Hotel Bombay.

Soon after this, word comes through that all Sudanese must return to Kakuma. UNHCR staff are adamant. Any Sudanese who chooses to remain in Dadaab will not be given rations or protection.

'Our hands are tied,' they tell those who protest. 'Your government has decided this is how it must be.'

Some react with anger. 'Are we just bundles of maize to be divided up and carted off wherever it pleases them to send us?'

'Dadaab is for Somalis,' the officials insist. 'Kakuma for Sudanese. We cannot support you here. You must go back.'

Some agree to go. Many do not. Obulejo decides to stay on. Business at the Hotel Bombay is brisk, and he and Maku get to eat at least once a day, sometimes twice. Their customers appreciate the meals they are able to purchase in the café. It's true he will be eligible for registration in Kakuma if he goes back, and will be given rations. But what use is that if the Rebels who have free entrance to the camp kidnap him and drag him back over the border?

'Why do you say no?' the UNHCR officials demand of those who refuse to go. 'If you choose to stay, don't come and complain to us. You will be on your own.'

More and more people register, board the buses and are borne away. Then an announcement comes that the buses will stop running in three weeks' time. A rush of people descends on the office. Staff members work frantically to register them. Obulejo feels a flicker of alarm. Nearly all Ma'di have left. Are Obulejo and Maku to be the only Ma'dis left in Dadaab?

Maku finally decides to go off to be registered for transfer to Kakuma. Obulejo is dismayed. This means the end of Hotel Bombay.

'Come with me,' Maku encourages Obulejo. 'We can still work together. And we will be among our own people. Among Christians.'

He still harbours a dream of completing his training for the priesthood.

When the last bus stands outside the compound, soon to depart, Obulejo finally accepts the inevitable and trudges to the UNHCR office. He registers just in time to get on that last bus.

The journey back is a bitter one for Obulejo. When he left Kakuma, he thought it was forever. Now he is returning in defeat.

The bus rumbles onwards, halting at checkpoints and stopping intermittently for rest stops and to refuel. The passengers jostle together, sometimes silently and sombrely, other times chatting among themselves, speculating on whether life will be less of a struggle in the new camp. Finally the bus trundles through the outskirts of the town of Kakuma and arrives at the camp.

Obulejo knows the drill by now. Temporary shelter, processing, being assigned barracks with yet another group, and then starting camp life all over again.

Suddenly a familiar voice calls his name. Obulejo looks up. A boy is pushing his way through the new arrivals, waving and beckoning excitedly. It's Ochan.

'Welcome, brother!' he calls.

Two other Acholis are with him, Longoya and Ochaya, who were choir members in Dadaab. They too are grinning and reaching out to shake Obulejo's hand. Then he spots Maku in the crowd as well.

'What took you so long, stubborn boy?' Maku asks him.

Obulejo has no answer.

Maku laughs and claps Obulejo on the back. 'Well, now you are among friends at least.'

'We can help each other,' the others assert.

Obulejo's spirits lift at this unexpected welcome.

It is not possible to survive alone in the refugee life, he knows. Friends are more precious than gold or diamonds.

19

THE NEXT FEW WEEKS pass slowly. Obulejo and his friends are eventually assigned a small plot of land on which to build a shelter. The first thing they decide is to pool their rations and endeavour to make their food last the full fortnight between distributions. They also decide to share income from any jobs they are able to secure.

Another housemate, a few years older than Maku, joins them: Santino, a Ma'di man. So now they are six: three Ma'dis, Obulejo, Maku and Santino, and three Acholis, Ochan, Longoya and Ochaya. 'The Six Musketeers,' Ochan dubs them. 'All for one and one for all!' For Obulejo, as for them all, this group will be 'family' in Kakuma.

The new household functions well, in the beginning. The Six Musketeers look out for each other and take turns to stand guard at night. They draw up a roster for cooking and housework, for collecting rations and standing in line for water. Maku and Ochan, both of whom hope to become priests, quickly become absorbed in church activities. Obulejo often joins them. Not only is he glad to see Father Angelo again, but the open-air church services also provide a familiar, safe setting, and music and dancing bring memories of home.

Back home he was known as a quiet and considerate boy, so he makes sure he is polite and accommodating to those he is sharing the shelter with. He fulfils his duties quietly and unobtrusively and tries not to get in the way. Most of the others are older than Obulejo and when they are all together he feels a bit shy. It is only in the daily prayer and choir sessions that he feels confident to stand up and teach a song or to lead the singing, when invited.

At night, the Musketeers chew over camp rumours, discuss hopes and fears and plans – for getting a job, for resettlement, for going home when all this is over. Sometimes they talk about home and their families, but not often, because then sadness descends too rapidly. Uchan and Maku sometimes talk about church matters. Obulejo says little; he has always been more of a listener than a talker. But he drinks in the conversation eagerly, in spite of his worries.

Even when there is no paraffin for the lamp, the Musketeers sit in the stuffy darkness for hours, talking. Obulejo listens to the occasional shout of laughter from Maku and the Acholi twang of Ochan, Longoya and Ochaya's speech, distinct from the familiar Ma'di rhythms of Maku and Santino. Ensconced in these gatherings Obulejo feels reassured and supported. It's an echo of home. A time in which they can forget the forces arrayed against them.

Sand and dust are big enemies, sifting in swathes through clothes and food and piling up against the walls of the shelters during the windstorms, blowing into faces. Everyone in Kakuma has red, inflamed eyes: children with gummed-up eyes play in the dust, babies stare through sticky lashes and elders sit in doorways with their backs to the whirling grit.

With only the nylon sheeting of their shelter with its bush poles and palm fronds tied over the roof as protection against the unceasing desert winds, Obulejo suffers from itchy eyes like everyone else. Then a night comes when he reaches for his share of the kidney beans and finds he cannot see where the dish is.

Finally his hand knocks against it and he manages to ladle out a portion. He is alarmed and embarrassed. Later that night when he tries to find his way out of the tent he bangs into one of the poles. He cannot see at all.

'What's wrong?' Ochan asks him.

'I don't know.' Obulejo can feel panic rising. 'I could see perfectly well during the day, but now I see nothing.'

The others cluster round, trying to reassure him.

'What is to become of me?' he cries. 'Ai-eeh!'

The boys lead him back into the tent. 'You must wait here. Stay still. And in the morning go and seek help in the clinic.'

All night long the wind blows hard, and the *boop boop boop* of the tent fabric as it billows out and flaps back, over and over, keeps pace with the anxious bumping of Obulejo's heart.

Next morning, he can see again, although his eyes are still sore. After waiting in line at the clinic for several hours, he is examined by a doctor.

'Night blindness,' the doctor says, matter-of-factly. 'Caused by lack of Vitamin A.'

He hands Obulejo a paper twist of vitamin pills. 'Take these and in a few days your sight will be restored.'

Obulejo is hugely relieved.

'And try to eat yellow and orange vegetables. That will stop the problem returning.' The doctor sighs. Getting hold of fruit and vegetables in Kakuma is well nigh impossible, as he and Obulejo both know.

When his sight is restored, worry still plagues Obulejo's mind. *How can I make sure of getting the right foods, to stop the blindness coming back?* he wonders, anxiously. *And what if I catch something even worse?*

If I don't stay healthy I'll never survive.

Obulejo decides to try to revive the Hotel Bombay in Kakuma. He approaches the others in his shelter, one by one, to partner with him, but they all say no. Longoya has a bicycle which he uses to transport people, or lends out for a small fee, Ochaya collects parcels and supplies and stands in the ration queues for others in return for a small percentage and Ochan helps him when he is not involved with church activities. Maku and Santino are also busy: Santino is attending a camp school and Maku is teaching at the same school and assisting the priests.

Obulejo is in the grip of the old dilemma. Be a compliant camp inmate, resigned to being simply one among the hundred and seventy thousand inmates of Kakuma who must queue for hours for poor food and dirty water that cause illness, or grasp whatever means he can to improve his lot. It's obvious what he must do. Stealing is wrong – yes. Bullying people is wrong – of course. But without them he might not survive.

The next day he singles out a target. A youth, not much older than himself, dressed in reasonably clean clothes, walking along a laneway, carrying a package. He must be one of the better-off inmates of Kakuma. The opportunity is too good to pass up. Obulejo quickens his step, till he is level with the young man, then reaches out and snatches the package.

Before the young man can attempt to grab it back, Obulejo turns his face into a threatening mask. 'Try it and I will beat you!' he hisses.

Then he turns tail and runs.

Too easy, he thinks, as he examines the contents of the package and strides off to a distant marketplace to exchange the clothing in the parcel for meat and bread.

Next, he repeats the old trick of causing a disturbance in the ration queue, so as to move himself further up the line, though he is careful not to recklessly draw the fire of the guards.

Each day presents new opportunities: food stored in flimsy shelters, just waiting to be filched, articles of clothing and household utensils left unguarded for a second, jerrycans over-burdened women have stashed at the water station to collect later.

Some things he sells, some he takes for his own use.

Despite his fear of kidnappers he takes care to range widely through the camp on his looting forays, lest he be recognised by those nearest to his shelter. But no one enquires too closely into his activities. Everyone in Kakuma has learned not to ask too many questions, and the others in Obulejo's household are busy with their own concerns.

How else is a boy on his own to survive? he asks himself. And he's not the only one using force, that's for sure. The Kenyan guards the UNHCR employ to safeguard the inmates can be brutal and threatening at times. Plus they allow the Rebels free rein in the camp.

It's all very well for the Kenyans, Obulejo thinks angrily. *They go back to their compounds at the end of each day and leave us at the mercy of marauders every night.*

Danger lurks in the most mundane tasks and situations. Violence simmers constantly. People are short-tempered, moody and irritable. Those who chew *miraa* or *khat* to block out reality in a narcotic dream are particularly prone to violent outbursts. Chewing the leaves is supposed to calm people, to take the edge off the nightmare of refugee life, but Obulejo can nearly always spot the users by their volatility and nervous excitability. They can swing from maundering passivity to screaming violence in the space of a few minutes.

One morning, as Obulejo is on his way to fetch water he sees five boys standing talking, their jerrycans lined up across the path. Suddenly a bicycle comes hurtling along carrying two Somali boys, one steering and the other balanced on the handlebars. The bicycle swerves and collides with the chattering boys, sending their jerrycans flying. The Somali boys giggle, their laughter high-pitched and drug-shrill.

'You useless dogs,' the boys yell at the riders. 'Why don't you look where you're going?'

'Out of our way, scum!' one of the Somali boys yells back. 'Why are you blocking the path anyway?' And he pushes the bike forward.

'Get back!' the Sudanese boys yell. One of them steps forward and grabs the handlebars. The other rider jumps off the bike and pulls out a knife. He lunges forward and plunges the knife into the boy's thigh. The rest of the boys rush to their friend's defence. The knife wielder strikes again. His victim falls to the ground. The screaming starts in earnest then.

Obulejo stands by, clutching his empty jerrycans, not knowing what to do. People come running, then. Knives flash, pangas are wielded, spears thrown and clubs and fists brandished. Obulejo turns tail and runs. There will be no extra water for their household today.

That afternoon, after prayers, people in the church square are talking about the incident. Fifty people were wounded and two killed. The main aggressors, it seems, were boy soldiers. No surprise there.

'They're a disgrace,' someone murmurs.

'They're animals,' another adds.

'No one is safe around them.'

'Especially our women and girls.'

Father Angelo interrupts. 'What else can you expect?' he says. 'They have been brought up without justice, under the rule of the gun. Their childhood has been stolen from them, their identity taken. Who has taught them culture or respect, or initiated them into manhood? What hope do they have for the future? They will never be able to raise a bride price.'

There is a moment's silence, before the debate starts up again. It rages furiously for several minutes. Father Angelo reminds them that all men are brothers, all the sons of God, and while no one openly contradicts the priest, Obulejo sees mutinous looks exchanged and hears sullen mutters. No one has a good word to say for the boy soldiers. When Father Angelo delivers the final blessing that day the response is somewhat muted.

It's all so hard to make sense of, Obulejo thinks as he settles down to sleep that night. Father Angelo's words repeat themselves in his mind. 'They have been brought up without justice and under the rule of the gun.'

I have been brought up by a wise father, good uncles and caring older brothers, Obulejo admits, *and yet I am turning to violence. Is this what war does to people?*

20

OBULEJO STILL LOVES the times when he can join others to sing and dance and praise God. When he loses himself in the shared rhythms of the *adungu* dance, his inner conflicts are set aside and for long minutes he is once more the honest, upright obedient son his father taught him to be, and no longer the violent thief Kakuma has turned him into.

But his favourite part of the day is when darkness falls and the members of his household sit together to talk, almost like real family. He feels closest to them at such times, and can almost forget the bad things he's done during the day.

One evening, Maku tells Obulejo about a course advertised at his school – an eight-week agricultural course run by the International Rescue Committee. It will be held after classes finish for the day, and is due to commence the following week.

'I think it would be good for you to enrol,' Maku says.

'Maybe,' Obulejo replies.

Maku expresses surprise at Obulejo's lack of enthusiasm.

'If you complete that course you might be able to get a job in one of the GTZ plant nurseries,' he says. 'It would be something to be part of the seedling distribution project.'

'Maybe,' Obulejo replies again.

He is not going to let his hopes rise unduly. In this refugee life he has learned that hope can be a dangerous drug. Anyway, it's not agriculture he wants to learn about; it's his intermediate certificate he wants to complete, then senior high. But with no money to buy paraffin for the lamp so he can read and study at night, and no money to buy books, any serious schooling is out of the question – just a dream – no longer real. The war has spoiled everything.

He must trim his dreams to fit his circumstances.

Stop wishing and face reality.

'There is no cost for the course,' Maku says, as if divining Obulejo's thoughts.

In spite of himself, Obulejo feels a small flame of hope begin to flicker. He savours the thought of being a student again. Perhaps he can even become a teacher himself one day! Then he pulls himself up short. The course is only two months long: what can he learn in eight weeks that will qualify him for anything, much less a teaching job?

'No. It is impossible,' he responds abruptly.

He sees the surprised look on Maku's face and feels ashamed. Is this how a good Ma'di boy should behave? Maku is offering advice as any older brother would and Obulejo is rudely refusing it. His father would be angry at this lack of respect.

'Very well,' Maku says quietly, 'but you might give it some thought.'

Obulejo spends that night in mental turmoil. It's Maku's fault, Obulejo tells himself. If Maku had reprimanded him, called him an ungrateful dog, a stupid boy, insisted he take his older brother's advice, Obulejo might not have turned his face away from the opportunity and wouldn't be lying here sleepless, with his stomach churning. He knows Maku is right. But why should he have to abandon his big dreams and settle for unwanted scraps?

Is there any point? His feet are already on the slippery path he has chosen. Around and around the argument circles in his mind. The course might lead nowhere. There's no guarantee it will gain him a job. Better to settle for the life he has. *Anyway, how can I attend a course unwashed and in rags?* he fumes. *I've got more chance of surviving as a thief!*

It's all very well for Maku, Obulejo thinks. *The church will take care of him.* Obulejo knows it's not that simple, nor is it even true, but it doesn't make him feel any less resentful. *As I have been robbed, so I will continue to rob others*, he concludes. *It is the only way open to me now.*

Surprisingly, Maku does not mention the course again but from that evening Obulejo feels that Maku is cooler to him. Perhaps he imagines it, but it seems as if a drop of poison as fatal as that traditionally smeared on Ma'di arrows is now infecting their household. And it is all his fault.

Uneasy months pass. Obulejo becomes an adept thief, more watchful, swift and devious, and much more aggressive. More like the boy soldiers, he realises with dismay. He understands better now how they feel – having their families and childhood stolen from them and being forced to kill others and then dumped into this worthless ragtag refugee existence. No wonder they stop at nothing – even the guards' Kalashnikovs. Not that he can waste pity on those boys; they would kill him without a second thought.

He tries not to think about what he has become, but even as he enjoys the extra rations his thieving gains him and is able to replace his threadbare T-shirt with one of better quality after a particularly successful raid, his disquiet grows. The camp, with its nightmare version of everyday life, is turning him into someone he no longer recognises.

His household is beginning to change too. At first the six of them shared everything and would spend long hours together each night. But now they all seem to be going their separate ways. The Musketeers' bonds are loosening.

Santino has a girlfriend and spends most of his time with her. Obulejo is jealous, although he knows that most of the Ma'di girls who gather for prayers and hymn-singing would not look twice at a ragged boy like himself. Besides, Santino is older and a man. And it is not so much Santino's girlfriend that makes Obulejo envious – Longoya and Ochaya have girlfriends too, laughing silly girls who peep coyly up at their Acholi beaus from under lowered lashes – it is because Santino is able to go to school. His family located him through the Red Cross and managed to transfer money to him so he can finish high school.

It's not fair. Santino has his family to help him and a girlfriend to look after him but Obulejo has nothing. His thieving might get him extra food but it doesn't get him the family he longs for or the education he craves. He tries to talk to Ochan about how desperately he wants to go back to school, but Ochan just tells him to trust God. *What good will that do*, Obulejo thinks sourly. God has forgotten him. Nothing will ever change.

Then suddenly it does.

Obulejo spots a notice advertising a second course in agriculture. The notice is attached to the perimeter wall of the school compound, which he often passes on his way to fetch water. He reads the notice and goes to turn away, but his legs seem to move of their own will into the school compound. They carry him straight to the admin office and within minutes he has filled out an application form.

As he retraces his steps, he begins to question his impetuous action. Eight weeks of farm studies will get him nowhere, and going to class every day will leave him less time to search for food. What's more, he will have to get up before dawn to collect water for showering and washing his clothes for class. And what about the chores at home? There are already arguments about those.

He pushes these thoughts out of his mind. It's done now, and only time will tell if he has made the right decision. At least his days will be spent with students, rather than in the dusty laneways of the camp scavenging for food, fighting off attacks or seeking out victims.

Keeping to the routine of regular classes will require determination. Can he do it? He has no choice but to try. He hurries home to tell Maku.

Maku is delighted. 'You have made the right decision,' he says. 'The course provides an opportunity and you are wise to take it.'

Obulejo is glad he has not told Maku about his thieving and bullying activities. He thinks of his family and the difficulties his father has faced throughout his life. What if there were things Baba had been forced to do so his family could survive, wrong things that he now regretted?

Right and wrong seemed so clear once, but the war has changed all that.

Now he must put all his energy into completing the course. A new path has appeared before him. He must follow where it leads.

On day one of the course, Obulejo arrives earlier than the other students. He is nervous. What if one of his victims is here and recognises him? What if his brain can only turn itself to stealing and cheating now, and no longer absorb information?

The first day is exhausting. How can he return, day after day, for eight long weeks, he wonders as he flops down to sleep that night. But he knows he will keep coming back.

No longer does Obulejo have the time or opportunity to scout for extra food. His stomach growls. And some days he is so exhausted after class that he can barely face the day's chores. The others are skimping on their duties too. Some days Obulejo comes home and finds the person rostered on for cooking absent, and no meal prepared. He must cook for himself then, and some nights he sits alone, churning over the same bitter thoughts, again and again. *These people are not my relatives. I am nothing to them. Will I be surrounded by strangers forever? Is this how my life will end, far from family, with only other refugees as companions?* Such thoughts sour his temper.

One day Ochan reminds Obulejo that it is his turn to prepare the meal.

'It's not,' Obulejo retorts.

'Yes it is,' Ochan replies.

'Anyway, even if it is my turn,' Obulejo says, 'I have cooked many times when it was your turn, or Ochaya's or Longoya's.'

'And now you must cook again,' Ochan replies.

'Why can't you cook for me today? Must I attend to my studies and perform women's work as well?'

Maku enters the argument then. 'Your agriculture classes do not begin until school ends at noon, so there is plenty of time to cook *and* get to the school compound on time.'

'Mind your own business,' Obulejo says. 'These Acholi dogs wish to treat me as their servant.'

The Acholi boys are furious. 'You insult our tribesmen! Apologise at once.'

'I will not!'

'Ma'di hyena!'

'Acholi snake!'

The boys glare at each other, fists clenched.

It is Maku who defuses the situation. 'I will cook today,' he says, 'and Ochan will assist me.'

All Obulejo's bluster evaporates.

'I wasn't meaning you should do my work,' he mutters.

Maku says nothing. He simply beckons Ochan and together they start to rinse the maize. The other Acholi boys leave. Obulejo is not sure what to do.

Later, Maku takes Obulejo aside. 'What is happening with you?' he asks quietly.

Obulejo does not reply. He cannot explain what it is that brings such bitter words to his lips, what makes him so wild with anger.

'I know it is hard,' Maku says, 'but we must try to live in peace together as best we can.'

Obulejo longs to unburden himself to Maku, to spill out all his fear and confusion, but something makes him hold his tongue. Trust nobody is the first rule of survival in a refugee camp. Besides, it would disappoint Maku to learn that Obulejo has fallen into bullying and stealing and that he cries like a small child for their Musketeer family that is not even family.

That night, in the darkness Obulejo again weeps silently, as he has done so many nights in Kakuma. Everything is such a mess. He will never be able to sort it out.

In the morning he tries to hide the signs of his night's distress from his housemates.

'Are you ill?' they ask him.

'It is nothing,' he replies.

He quickly volunteers to go for the water. Anything to get him out of the shelter till he can calm himself again. He plods his way to the resource centre closest to the school compound. The trucks have not yet arrived so Obulejo sinks to the ground, his head bowed. He sits there, unmoving, for a long time. After a while, anger begins to replace sorrow. Anger at the others, at first, but then more strongly towards himself. How could he have acted so badly? Especially to Maku, who is like an older brother. And to Ochan, his old schoolfriend.

Are you a child that you cannot control yourself? he berates himself.

Fear starts to squeeze his heart into a hard knot. *You'll soon see*, he tells himself, *they will cast you out! 'Your behaviour is not good. Get out from here.' That is what they will say. They don't have to put up with you. You have no claim on them, or they on you.*

None of the Musketeers is from the same clan, while Ochan and Longoya and Ochaya are not even from the same tribe. They cannot replace true family – parents, to whom a child is precious beyond price and who love their children their whole lives, older brothers who show the younger ones the right way to live, sisters who care, aunties and uncles who teach and nurture and protect – even though they have promised to stand up for each other.

It was from Uncle Sylvio Obulejo first heard the story of the Three Musketeers and the young d'Artagnan who joined them to fight loyally against evil and injustice. If only *his* musketeers could be so loyal!

Obulejo remembers Uncle at the fireside after supper, telling that story. He was the best storyteller of all; he made everybody laugh and cry and gasp out loud, and he knew stories from all over the world, as well as the traditional stories of his own people.

In his mind's eye Obulejo sees his family gathered around the fire, the night sky studded with stars and flames casting pools of light on Uncle's dark skin and on the faces of the listeners, the elders sipping sweet tea, his little sister Izia sleeping in her mother's skirts and young Amoli curled up like a puppy next to Obulejo, listening, spellbound, as the big people talk and tell stories.

Amoli loves *The Three Musketeers* too. Every time Uncle gets to 'All for one and one for all!' Amoli shouts it out with him, and the grown-ups laugh loudly. Everyone loves the story about the band of brothers in faraway France, overcoming evil. *Perhaps French people aren't that different from us*, Obulejo thinks: 'all for one and one for all' is nearly the same as the 'one door' – *joti alu kaka* – for Ma'di families.

But Uncle is gone, killed by the Rebels, and the family is scattered. It's been a long time since he saw any of them and no word of their fate has come to him, no message. They are lost to him, perhaps forever.

But worse than the absence of his family is the knowledge that his parents would hardly recognise the boy they once knew. They would be ashamed of what he has become.

21

OBULEJO DOESN'T WANT to admit to Maku that he sees no point in anything, so he just keeps on attending his classes. Besides, the course gives him something to do other than fight and steal and attack others, even if some days he just sits in class like a basking alligator, absorbing nothing.

If the older brothers were around they would discuss the course with him, and ask him about the things he is learning. At home, education is what everyone talked about most of the time. For as far back as he can remember Obulejo has enjoyed watching and listening to his father earnestly discussing school and college assignments with the older brothers.

'Education is the way forward for our people,' he has heard his father say a thousand times.

It has always been taken for granted that all nine children in the family would go to school and Moini has worked hard to pay school and college fees for his sons and daughters.

Obulejo remembers how eagerly he waited for it to be his turn to start school. And when the day came at last, he set out in clean new shorts and shirt, with sharpened pencils and a crisp new exercise book, breathless with excitement. He would learn how to read and then all the enticing secrets in his big brothers' books would be his. He recalls only too well the crushing disappointment of discovering, after struggling for hours all that first day with the twisty Arabic characters, that he still was unable to read. He'd run home weeping and Moini had laughed when he heard the reason.

'You must have patience, my son. The skill of reading will be yours in time, I promise.'

And it happened just as his father promised. When the older brothers next came home from college and university on vacation how proudly Obulejo demonstrated his new skill to them! The brothers rewarded him with juicy chunks of sugar cane. He can still taste the sweet juice on his lips and tongue.

'You have made a good start,' his brothers praised him. 'Now you must continue to work hard at your studies so that you will become an educated, responsible adult. Remember, if you want a door to open, education is the key.'

Obulejo promises himself that he will complete the agricultural course. It will be difficult, in the harsh conditions of the camp, but he will do it.

One of the worst problems he faces, as a student in Kakuma, is the ferocious daytime heat. He finds it almost impossible to concentrate. At night there's not enough light in the shelter to read by. His solution is to wait till the late afternoon when the air becomes cooler, and to complete his reading and assignments then.

As he puts all his energies into his studies he starts to feel less burdened. He sets off for the school compound each day feeling that he is shrugging himself back into his own skin for the first time since that day on the hillside above Torit. Little by little, he warms to the course. It's intriguing to compare what he is learning now with the traditional methods his family and clan have always used to grow their food.

Becoming a student again reawakens his fierce desire to complete his interrupted school studies. He wonders whether Juma has finished high school yet. Perhaps he is already in Cairo with Lino and Jaikondo. Lucky Juma!

Round and round in his mind, Obulejo chases a solution. School is free, in the camp, but there are books and other materials to be purchased, seven subjects to study for the intermediate certificate, assignments to complete and exams to pass. All that and water and rations to collect, wood for the cooking fires to gather, household chores to be done – and this in the unsettled, often dangerous surroundings of the camp.

He'll have to get a job. It's the only way, if he wants to continue his schooling. But he can hardly work and study at the same time. There aren't enough hours in the day.

But he must not go back to his former ways. He wants to be an educated man, a good man, not someone lost in wickedness and crime, like some of the boys in the camp who do not attend school.

Grandfather always used to say, 'An idle mind is the workshop of the devil.'

Perhaps if he works hard, he can achieve what he desires.

Perhaps he can find a way.

Increasingly Obulejo is spending more time alone in the shelter. Weary from a day of studying, reading and assignment writing, he often comes home to an empty tent. Maku and Ochan are bound up in church and school duties and nearly every evening Santino is out drinking, playing cards and dominoes with his friends, or visiting his girlfriend. Longoya and Ochaya are hardly ever home either. They spend most of their free time with their girlfriends, or other young men in the Ma'di sector. Pretty girls are all they talk about. Obulejo is now nearly seventeen, and he's interested in girls too, but he tells himself he cannot think of such things yet; first he must find a way to continue his education. Girlfriends can come later.

Every day of the agricultural course he enters the school compound and passes the main office, where enrolments are taken. And every day he thinks, *if only I could stay longer than the eight weeks of my course.* Being in a school compound feels so familiar, so right. Then one day he comes home hugging a delicious secret, an idea that came to him unexpectedly. Maybe the spirit of his father visited him in his sleep and whispered in his ear. Whatever the reason, the idea is here, firmly lodged in his mind, and now he only has to summon the will to put it into action.

Next day, with barely a week of classes left, he finds himself stepping onto the verandah of the school admin building, pushing open the door of the office and walking in. Whole flocks of butterflies stir frenziedly in his stomach as he waits quietly for the receptionist's attention.

At last she looks up. 'Yes?'

Obulejo has gone over and over what he will say, but when it comes to the point his carefully rehearsed speech flies out of his head. He stands, mute.

'Yes?' the receptionist says again. She taps the edge of her pen against her teeth, impatiently.

'Excuse me, madam,' Obulejo says. 'May I see one of the principals?'

He feels shame for his tattered clothes, his dusty legs and feet. He fully expects the woman to tell him to stop wasting her time and go away.

'Wait here,' she says and disappears. A few minutes later she returns. 'Principal Kamau will see you now.'

What do you think you are doing? a mocking voice in his head whispers as he makes his way to Principal Kamau's office. *You're just a boy, and a ragged one at that.*

But a second voice is whispering, *Take courage.*

He decides that this is the one he will heed.

A tall, skinny man with grizzled hair is standing by the window.

'I'd like to offer my services as a voluntary teacher,' Obulejo blurts out, lowering his eyes.

He explains breathlessly. 'I have been able to attend a short course. But I cannot continue because I can't afford to buy paraffin for reading and studying at night. I completed junior and was in intermediate before I came to Kakuma, and I think I could teach the younger students. I ask no salary, just the opportunity to be part of your school.'

Principal Kamau is silent. Is he surprised? Angry? Obulejo waits anxiously for a response.

'I commend you for your offer,' the principal says at last. 'Never before have I met a person so passionate about education that he would offer to teach others and ask no payment for it.'

The principal looks out of the window for a moment, then goes back to his desk. Obulejo's heart falls. Is he going to be refused?

After another moment of silence, Principal Kamau says, 'What subjects do you think you are capable of teaching?'

Obulejo's heart leaps, but he answers calmly, politely. 'Science, business education and history were my strongest subjects, sir.'

The principal strokes his chin.

At last he says, 'I'll speak to the other teachers.'

Obulejo's heart is beating so hard he thinks it might burst through his chest wall.

'Thank you, sir,' he stammers, and leaves the office.

Will Principal Kamau and the other teachers agree? Who can tell. Whatever happens, he is glad he listened to the inner voice that told him to step up and take courage.

Ten days later Obulejo and his fellow students are presented with their graduation certificates. Having completed the agricultural course with high marks, Obulejo is free now to try his hand at teaching! Principal Kamau and the other teachers have agreed to give him a trial. He can hardly believe his luck.

He is assigned a science topic to prepare and present to one of the junior classes. Principal Kamau and three other teachers will observe from the back of the classroom, and if Obulejo conducts the lesson well, he will be taken on as a voluntary staff member.

The topic he is assigned is the human digestive system, something he studied at St Xavier's, and with a bit of effort Obulejo is able to recall most of what he was taught, more than two years ago. But just to make sure, he consults the small collection of textbooks in the makeshift school library and prepares diagrams and a set of quiz questions to test the students with at the end of his presentation.

He enters the crowded classroom nervously. 'Today we are going to be thinking about food,' he begins.

Dozens of faces stare back at him.

'What better topic can there be for a refugee?' he continues. 'I am sure you are all interested in food, aren't you?'

Most grin shyly. A few look hostile.

Step by step Obulejo leads the pupils through the lesson. He draws diagrams on the board so they can picture what goes on inside their own bodies. Sixty wriggling students soon become intrigued. When it is time for the quiz, Obulejo glances round the class to make sure everyone is paying attention, then puts the first question. 'Where does the process of digestion begin?'

Sixty pairs of eyes stare back at him. Sixty tongues remain mute. He scans the class again. Have they heard? Did they understand? Has he explained the lesson well enough?

'Look at the diagram on the board,' he tells them. Then he points to a small boy whose feet barely reach the floor.

'Can you give me the answer?'

The boy stares at Obulejo, then slowly raises one hand to his lips.

Obulejo nods encouragingly. 'Correct. The mouth. Digestion begins in the mouth.'

'What is the scientific word for chewing?' he asks next.

'Ma-sti-ca-tion,' another child ventures hesitantly.

So far so good.

'What does saliva do?'

One or two raise their hands, offer halting explanations.

'Explain peristalsis.'

'What is the function of the stomach acids?'

More and more hands are raised. Children are soon leaping to their feet as Obulejo points to them, and their answers come thick and fast, some of them correct, some not. Patiently Obulejo goes over the things they get wrong. At last the lesson is over.

Principal Kamau and Obulejo leave the classroom together. 'You have a gift for education, my friend,' Principal Kamau tells Obulejo. 'And you have a good spirit. You are going to be an inspiration for others.'

The principal's words feel like treasures beyond price to Obulejo. Thank goodness he summoned the courage to present his proposal. To find a way that helps others and will also make his own life better is the real prize. And he has found it.

I am no longer the small boy who feared the terrible baboons so dreadfully, he realises, as he leaves the school compound that day. *I am finally learning to be brave, in my own particular way.*

And when he is informed that he has indeed been accepted as a teacher, Obulejo's joy knows no bounds.

He is assigned a large group of younger children, to whom he will teach most of the basic subjects. Obulejo sets to with a will. His classes are mostly held outside, under a tree, with only an improvised blackboard and a few textbooks. He spends hours preparing sums and word lists for his class, and writing out the words of songs to use in reading lessons.

It is surprisingly hard work being a teacher, he soon discovers. Some of his students seem unable to take in what he is trying to teach them, no matter how many times or how carefully he explains. It's as though their minds are closed doors.

Some gaze vacantly into space or nod drowsily, heads bowed over their crossed arms. Sometimes the only way he can rouse them is to set up a circle game and get them to count as they throw the ball to each other.

A few of the students are rowdy and disruptive. He thinks of these as the *lore* of the class. He cannot run away from them, so he has to find a way to tame them. They show him none of the deference he gave his own teachers. These are troubled times and many of the old ways have been swept away by war. Besides, he is only a few years older than some of his students; he cannot expect to receive the same respect the students give Principal Kamau and the more experienced teachers.

He introduces activities that he hopes will engage his students and harness their restless energy. His greatest success is with music. Obulejo loves to sing and dance, so each day he leads the class in a series of songs and gets them to beat out the rhythm with their hands, while he points to each line of the song on the blackboard.

'Today we are going to sing about the sun waking up,' he tells his students one morning.

He sings the song for them, pausing at the end of each line so they can repeat it after him. After they have run through the song a few times he calls a little girl out to the front and hands her a card with the English word 'sun' on it.

'Now we will sing once more,' he tells his pupils, 'and this time, when we get to the word "sun", Abeba will hold her card up so everyone can see it.'

He chooses ten more children and gives each of them a card. Some of the children giggle and shuffle and drop their cards, chew the corners or hold them upside down. Some swap cards with each other, but even the most recalcitrant students gain a few new words.

Obulejo loves to see the students' eyes sparkle with interest and to know that they've been momentarily transported out of this hot, dusty place. He vows that one day he will complete his own education, and perhaps become a qualified teacher.

THERE ARE DAYS when nothing goes right, when everyone is hot and tired and even the most willing students seem unable to grasp what Obulejo is trying to teach them, but he perseveres, and little by little the students progress.

He now has a new problem, though – lack of time. He must arrive at school clean and well-presented, so sometimes he has to get up at four a.m. and walk three miles or more to fetch the extra water he needs for bathing and washing his clothes. If he oversleeps he will find himself at the end of the queue: that means risking being late for work, which is unthinkable.

Sometimes Obulejo has good luck – if he arrives early enough at the resource centre near the school one of the watchmen allows him to get water there. Most of the watchmen will let the teachers use the tap in the compound, but only one at a time. If a watchman refuses him entry, Obulejo must wait till school is over and face a long weary trek to find water somewhere else.

In Kakuma, everyone thinks constantly about water. It is always in short supply. Many times Obulejo has seen young people loiter at the water collection point, waiting to see who has brought more than one jerrycan, and who is filling two or three at once, but can take only one home at a time – often women with babies and small children. When a woman sets off with her first jerrycan, leaving the others behind to collect on her return, the boys will grab one of them and pour the water into their own, then throw her empty can away. Obulejo has done it himself, many times in the past.

One day when everything has gone wrong and he is in a great rush, Obulejo notices two full jerrycans standing unattended near the water collection point. He glances about to see if anyone is watching and before he can stop himself he quickly upends one of the full jerrycans into his empty one. He then hurls the emptied can as far away as possible and dashes back to his shelter with the stolen water. At first he congratulates himself on his cleverness, but soon he becomes troubled by the mental image of a dismayed woman returning to collect her second load of water only to find part of it stolen – water she desperately needs for her family, perhaps even for some of the children in Obulejo's class.

Another day, something happens that leaves him with even greater shame and regret. It's a day when Obulejo must collect water and when he is also rostered on to cook for his household.

It is exam time and all the teachers have been told they must mark fifty papers each before they leave. They line up in groups to receive their allotted papers. The process is slow. Obulejo starts to get anxious. He approaches Principal Kamau and is given permission to swap to the first group. Even so, there are fifteen people ahead of him in the line. Obulejo gets more and more frantic. Finally he attempts to push his way in. The nearest man in the line resists. Obulejo's frustration boils over. He slaps the man, sharply. The principal frowns and calls Obulejo over.

'You have acted violently,' he says. 'You, a teacher. I am ashamed of you.'

Obulejo quickly apologises, but the stern look stays on the principal's face.

'You will wait till last to receive your papers,' he tells Obulejo, 'and then you will stay behind and mark them.'

By the time Obulejo gets home, impossibly late, Ochan has prepared their meal.

'Where have you been?' Ochan demands. 'Why should I do your work, you worthless boy?'

Obulejo tries to explain.

'Not good enough,' Ochan retorts.

The others are furious as well.

'Teacher get kept back for being a naughty boy?' Longoya taunts.

'Must we wait till midnight for our meal?' Ochaya adds.

Even Maku is angry with Obulejo.

But worse than the Musketeers' displeasure is the knowledge that the other teachers will now think badly of him. Perhaps they will decide he is no longer worthy to teach in the school.

The following day Principal Kamau calls Obulejo into his office. 'I cannot stress how deeply I disapprove of your actions yesterday,' he says. 'It is not only the lack of respect to your colleague I regret, but the poor example it sets for others.'

Now he will be told he can no longer teach, Obulejo thinks, but what Principal Kamau says next surprises him.

'The other teachers regret your actions too. But overall they consider you a valued colleague and wish to offer you support. They are waiting to meet with you in the staffroom right now.'

Obulejo can hardly believe his eyes when a fellow teacher hands him an envelope containing a brief note: *This will help you.* The note is signed by each of his colleagues, even the man he slapped, and the envelope contains money.

One of his colleagues steps forward. 'We, your fellow teachers, have decided to contribute a small proportion of our salaries each month to you,' he says. 'This will enable you to balance the procuring of necessary food and water supplies with the heavy demands of a teacher's life.'

Obulejo is speechless.

'We realise how difficult it has been for you,' the man goes on, 'and we believe you should be offered some recompense for your efforts.'

Obulejo is close to tears. Such generosity! And not a single mention of the exam paper incident.

'This gift touches me deeply,' he says in a low voice. 'It will help me improve my life and the lives of our students.'

And from this day on, he vows silently, *for the honour of my family and in the name of the Father in heaven, I will seek out peaceful ways.*

No more use of force to get my way.

Now Obulejo makes the trek to the school compound each day with a lighter heart.

His journeys back home are not so cheerful. The unwelcome truth is that his household is on the verge of collapse.

First the Acholi boys leave, one after the other. Obulejo is sorry to see Ochan, Longoya and Ochaya go. He knows he and Ochan will see each other regularly at church gatherings, but it will be hard to start again with new housemates. Maku says he will ask around for other people to join them, but days pass and nothing happens. Perhaps he too is preparing to leave; Santino as well. Obulejo realises that his substitute family soon will be no more.

One day, Obulejo is called to Principal Muraya's office. *Have I done something else wrong?* he wonders. But his fears are soon put to rest.

'You have been with us for four months now,' Principal Muraya says, 'and Principal Kamau and I wish to commend you for your dedication and good work.'

He smiles encouragingly and hands Obulejo a document.

Obulejo reads it over and over, until the magic words *You are now appointed as a teacher in this school* begin to waver and blur on the page. The blood roars in his ears as Principal Muraya congratulates him. Obulejo stutters his thanks and backs out of the office, almost falling down the steps.

He clutches the precious document and scans it a dozen times as he walks back to his dwelling. He is to teach the three subjects he nominated: science, business education and history – a full teaching load. And he will get a monthly stipend! Not a full salary like a trained teacher back home, but still a miracle. Without even finishing high school, somehow he has managed to become a teacher!

At the next church gathering Obulejo sings with a glad and grateful heart:

'Father, thank you for your grace – oh hallelujah!
For helping us to run life's race – oh hallelujah!
For your blessings great and small – oh hallelujah!

As each day on us they fall – hallelujah, hallelujah, halle-e-lu-jah!'

And when the dancing starts he is the first to leap to his feet. The lilting *adungus* accompany the song of happiness that dances inside him, and he feels something loosen, like a spring held tightly for too long beginning to uncoil. Perhaps the worst is over. His physical scars are becoming less livid, the wounds gradually reducing to raised weals on his smooth skin, and the dignity and sense of purpose in teaching is beginning to do the same for his inner scars.

He must do the best he can with the opportunity he has been given, and if it is in God's plan, one day his family will discover where he is and find a way to bring him home.

With his first month's modest pay Obulejo buys two nearly new T-shirts from a market in the nearby Kuku area, and a pair of trousers. He imagines his father's approving smile as he dons his new clothes, and he can't help swaggering a little as he sashays off to school the next day. It's as though he has leapt fully into manhood, and it's worth forgoing extra rations to feel less like a scarecrow. From now on he won't be forced to wash his clothes every single day, which means he'll be able to spend extra time preparing his classes. And he can teach his students and attend church better dressed and more confident.

Tuesdays and Saturdays are when all the young people practise their singing and music. Maku has set up a choir and he and Ochan take turns conducting the singers and players. The Sunday church services are getting more popular and people from other sectors often join in now – Congolese,

Ethiopians and even some of the Kenyan UNHCR staff. The hymns in Father Angelo's tattered hymn books are not so popular, though, especially with the Ma'dis. The tunes are dreary and the songs are all in Swahili or English. So each week Maku asks one of the young people to teach a song in Arabic, Lingala, the language of the Congo, or Ma'di.

'Today, we are going to learn to sing the Lord's Prayer in Ma'di,' Maku announces. This is one of Obulejo's favourites. He's sung it for as long as he can remember, both at home in the mountain village and at school in Torit.

'We will ask Obulejo and Malia to lead the choir today,' Maku says. 'They will teach you the words and the tune.'

He nods to a Ma'di girl standing with her friends at the edge of the group, and the girl steps forward shyly. Obulejo has seen her around; she's younger than him, maybe fourteen, a quiet girl with striking eyes and a sweet face. Together they hum the tune to the *adungu* players, and then turn to face the singers.

'Ama ata bua rii
nya ru kolu ole
opi nyidri kamu'

'Our Father who art in heaven, hallowed be thy name, thy kingdom come,' they sing in unison, pausing at the end of each line so the choir can repeat it after them. Their voices go well together. The choir quickly pick up the words and the tune, and the prayer rings out joyously in the shimmering afternoon. Obulejo is flushed and happy. He smiles at Malia and she smiles back. A tiny smile, but a smile, nevertheless. His heart skips a beat.

Next choir practice Obulejo arrives earlier than usual. He pretends to be absorbed in watching the *adungu* players fashion new instruments from bendy tree branches and then measure twine for the strings, but really he is looking out for Malia.

Maku asks him to lead the choir again that day. From time to time Obulejo steals glances at Malia. Whenever he catches her eye, she looks down. Then, in the dancing, he turns suddenly and their eyes meet. Malia immediately drops her gaze. But with a jolt of joy Obulejo realises this girl is interested in him. He knows he has to be careful. Strict rules govern friendships between boys and girls. After prayers, when people stand about catching up with one another, he and Malia are able to talk together casually, but when older people approach they quickly move apart.

One day, after the service, Malia asks him, 'What time are you going to fetch water?'

'Very soon,' Obulejo replies.

'I am also going to get water,' Malia says, with downcast eyes.

Obulejo tries to conceal his glee. 'Then I will accompany you,' he says. 'It is safer that way.'

The two speak little on the long walk to the tanks or on the way back, but Obulejo counts this as one of his best days ever in Kakuma.

Soon they are presented with other opportunities to be together. Until now, church services have been conducted under a tree. This gives the worshippers little shelter from the heat, the wind and the dust, but soon the young people will be undertaking a new project – erecting a makeshift church. It will be a big job, but Obulejo will be able to work alongside Malia while they do it!

Father Angelo praises the young people for their initiative. 'You know how burdened I feel for you,' he says, 'the 'unaccompanied minors' in Kakuma – young people on their own, without family – and how much I long to help you. But now you are helping yourselves and this excellent initiative will give you something to be proud of and show you what an important part of the church's spiritual family you are.'

Obulejo volunteers to be part of the construction group, along with Malia and her older sister Mondua and most of the other young people. Maku will oversee the work. They will use flattened metal oil tins for the roof, supported by poles supplied by the UNHCR or swapped with the local Turkana tribesmen for rations. They beg empty oil containers from people in their area and when they have gathered a large enough quantity they come together to open up and smooth out the tins. They then fold the edges of each tin into the next one and bash the edges tightly together with a stone. The roof-support poles are then set up and the strips of tin laid on smaller branches and nailed down. The tin roof will hold the heat in, unfortunately, but at least it will provide some protection for the worshippers.

Next, they chip one side of a number of long poles till the surface is relatively flat, then they set forked sticks into the earth and lay each pole on top, flat side up, to create benches for the churchgoers. All the while they are working Obulejo is intensely conscious of Malia close by. Her presence makes him edgy and excited but he is careful not to catch her eye or approach her while her sister is near.

Some girls sneak off at night to meet their boyfriends, he knows, and in some ways he admires couples brave enough to take that risk, but he would never expect Malia to put herself in such danger. If their friendship is to continue then he must act honourably, enjoy the times he is able to be near her and trust God's plan for the future. Meanwhile he enjoys the fizz and tingle he feels every time he catches sight of Malia.

The completed church shelter is named St Bakhita's, in honour of the Sudanese woman who fought for justice long ago, and was canonised by the Pope.

'Her suffering honours your own,' Father Angelo declares, at the consecration service.

During the celebrations afterwards, Obulejo dances as close as he dares to Malia, keeping an eye out for her sister. Then Mondua swings past and smiles at Obulejo and his heart lifts. She knows, he realises, and she is signalling her permission for his friendship with Malia to continue. Life suddenly feels much sweeter.

23

ONE PARTICULARLY HOT day, as the teachers sit fanning themselves at a staff meeting, the discussion turns to dealing with the challenging behaviour of some of their students. Caning is the traditional solution, both for bad behaviour and if students fail to recite their lessons correctly, but this isn't working for some pupils. Then there are the fights that constantly break out in the playground; these often result in serious injuries and are a great cause of concern. How are the teachers to prevent playground fights when the children constantly witness the violence of adults in the camp?

'Nothing we've tried has worked,' one teacher says dispiritedly.

'These students are angry, and without hope,' a senior teacher says. 'Their lives have been destroyed by the conflicts of their elders. Some may never recover.'

Obulejo nods. What hope can there be for homeless, stateless, hungry children, trapped in Kakuma as they are, with one hundred and seventy thousand other desperate souls, and everybody at each other's throats?

There seems to be no solution, but after mass one Sunday, Obulejo hears talk of a new program being run by the

UNHCR. His ears prick up. Something called P-E-P. What can it be? He edges closer, to learn more.

'What is this P-E-P?' he asks one of the elders.

'Peace Education Program,' the elder tells him. 'It teaches a way of living that does not lead to fighting. We all know that if children are surrounded by violence they will learn to be violent themselves, but the peace education program shows people how to solve conflicts with co-operation and respect, not fighting.'

Everyone starts to talk at once. The babble is deafening.

The elder holds his hand up for the crowd's attention. 'When they met with us they told us, "Having experienced so much conflict, you are the experts on peace."'

There is a collective indrawing of breath, a soft 'Ai-eeh'.

Obulejo is avid to know more. And when flyers appear, calling for people to be trained in peace education, he is one of the first to apply.

At the interview, his heart sinks a little when he is introduced to the panel members, a white woman from Australia and two Kenyans. Are foreigners to be in charge? Foreigners have ruled his fate since he left Sudan. But no, the elders have been consulted, and it is at their request the peace education program is to go ahead.

Three questions are put to Obulejo: 'What is your understanding of peace? Why do you want to do this training? What will you bring to the program?'

Obulejo considers his answers carefully. 'The thing that brought me into the refugee camp is war,' he says, 'but we all want peace. And to have peace, all of us need to participate. Peace to me is a process to which all people contribute. And that's why I feel I have something to contribute.'

The interviewers nod. Next he is presented with an imaginary scenario of a violent conflict, and asked how he would help the people involved find a solution.

'A woman is asking for help,' he is told. 'She goes from person to person, but no one will help her. Some brush her off without a word, others become angry. They shout at the woman, "Go away! You are bringing trouble to us when we have troubles of our own." The woman continues to cry for help. She has lost her child, but no one will help her. Hearing the shouting and weeping, other people approach. One man is shouting at the woman to go away, she is not his country-woman. Another accuses him of being hard-hearted. People begin to take sides and a fight breaks out.'

The interviewer pauses. 'Now how would you help the people to find a solution?' she asks Obulejo.

'What I would do . . .' Obulejo begins hesitantly, then pauses, gathers his thoughts and continues more confidently. 'Well, if I didn't know how the fighting started, I would talk it through with the people involved and get a sense of what exactly caused them to argue. I would ask them to listen to what the woman was saying and see if there was any way they could help her.'

'Good. Yes,' the white woman says. 'And would you then come up with a solution for them?'

Obulejo is silent for a few seconds. At last he says, 'Well, I'd ask them what they think. "Is it good if we keep on fighting each other? Will that fighting help us or help this woman?" I'd try, with my knowledge, to help them find the solution. I'd get to the solution through what they think and want.'

The interviewers consider his answer for a few moments, then smile at Obulejo. They thank him for attending the interview.

'We will let you know our decision as soon as possible,' he is told.

Within a week Obulejo learns that he has been accepted into the training program. He is overjoyed.

Memories of his flight to Kenya, his struggles in both Kakuma and Dadaab, his successes and failings flash past him. But what rings even more clearly in his mind are Moini's words, spoken so often through all the years of Obulejo's growing up: that everybody should be treated as though they were family. Perhaps this peace education program will show them how it can be done.

The training sessions take place when school ends in the early afternoon. The first day, Obulejo and his fellow trainees gather together under a dusty flame tree. Mondua is among them, Obulejo notices, feeling suddenly self-conscious and even more anxious about the program. Whatever the trainers have in store for them, an added pressure for Obulejo will be his desire to make a good impression on Malia's sister.

When they are told that everybody involved must first make a promise to be open and honest, Obulejo's heart skips a beat. What the trainer is asking is impossible. There are people here from many different tribes and countries. All have been involved in conflict. To be open and honest among enemies is pure foolishness, surely?

When he looks up, he sees the trainer smiling. 'From your perplexed expressions, I realise many of you will think this is not possible,' she says. 'But, believe me, there can be no peace without it.'

She asks each member of the group to recall an occasion in their lives when they co-operated with, or received friendship from, someone outside their own family, and to think about how it felt, and what resulted.

'Now turn to the person next to you and tell them the story,' she instructs.

Obulejo's mind instantly flies to Dadaab and setting up the Hotel Bombay with Maku, then to Deng helping him, Ochan and Loding escape from the Rebel barracks and guiding them across the Kenyan border, but when it comes time to swap stories with Nhial, the Nuer man with whom he is partnered, he finds himself recalling instead the day he broke one of his front teeth when he was just a young boy, back in the mountain village.

'Despite the tension between the Lotuko and the "foreigners" who lived and worked on Lotuko ancestral land, the children of Ma'di and other tribes had many Lotuko friends,' Obulejo tells Nhial. 'My best friend was Riti, a Moro boy, and we used to go fishing with our Lotuko friends all the time and play soccer together when we weren't doing chores. Sometimes we had play fights, and we also used to dare each other to do things – climb tall trees or hop from rock to rock or straddle a tree trunk across a wild stream.'

Nhial smiles. Perhaps he is thinking of his own childhood back in the Nuer lands.

'Well, one day Riti challenged me to rock-hop across a really fast-flowing river. I remember that day so well. I took a flying leap and landed on a rock that was covered in slime

172

and my feet slipped out from under me. Smack! I came down on my face on the rock. Didn't I yell!

'I thought I was a goner but the others jumped in to drag me out. Riti got to me first, though, and half dragged, half carried me home, apologising all the way. I'd smashed one of my front teeth and ai-eeh, didn't it hurt! The Lotuko boys rushed ahead yelling for help and when Riti and I got there they just stood round like stunned owls while Mama Josephina patched me up and shouted curses at them.

'I remember my father being angry at first but when Mama Josephina kept on about my broken tooth and "those treacherous and foolhardy Lotuko boys", my father said that far from being treacherous the Lotuko lads had shown me true friendship and it was in fact Riti who had led me into trouble, and did she blame the Moro, as well as the Lotuko, for her son's troubles, when Riti and the other boys had cared for him like a brother?

'"I forbid you to teach our children to speak badly of the Lotuko, when we are guests in their land," he told Mama, "and remember, if you try to keep a son swaddled in his mother's skirts forever he will never become a man."

'When I met up with Riti again in Torit,' Obulejo continues, 'we greeted each other as brothers. Riti touched his own front teeth and pointed to my damaged tooth and said, "Oh, so sorry," again and again in such a sad voice that I almost felt it was Riti who had been injured, not me.'

'Thus are the bonds of friendship formed from misfortune,' Nhial remarks, when Obulejo pauses.

Obulejo nods.

Nhial then gestures towards a Dinka trainee deep in conversation with a Nuer man. 'And it is true that friendship between enemies is possible.'

When Obulejo goes home that night his head is spinning with ideas and possibilities. He feels both inspired and confused, and today was just a taste of what's to come.

He and the other trainees are required to participate in many different activities – brainstorming sessions, role-play, games and practical exercises.

The trainers encourage them to give each other support and to work as a unit. Obulejo finds he is soon able to lose his self-consciousness about the impression he may be making on Mondua: he, along with everyone in the group, is too intent on learning how to create this new possibility – peace.

At first, some of the exercises seem rather childish to Obulejo, but he soon discovers that even skipping requires a high degree of concentration and co-operation. When two skippers trip in a tangle of rope and tumble into the dust, Obulejo and his group have to work out how to improve. They finally get a smooth rhythm going and six people have successfully skipped through the whirling ropes when the instructor calls a halt.

Obulejo and his partners grin at one another, triumphantly.

'Well done!' they tell each other.

'You turned the rope smoothly and regularly.'

'You jumped high and did not trip.'

'You made room for the skipper entering.'

'You ran out skilfully and did not tangle yourself in the rope.'

'You swung the rope high and in a good easy rhythm.'

Obulejo observes a similar jubilation among other groups of skippers. It's such a simple thing, but it has everybody smiling and praising each other, even those who are a little out of breath.

Next they play a relay game: the person at the head of the line runs out the front and throws the ball to the next person, then runs to the back of the line. Each team member must follow suit. Obulejo's team includes men and women of various ages and from four different tribes. They quickly learn that if they want their team to win they must be helpful and encouraging rather than critical of one another.

Another time the trainees are asked to stand in a circle, facing the male trainer in the centre. He tells them he is going to name an activity and then invite all those who enjoy that activity to step forward into the circle.

'Basketball.'

Smiles pass between group members.

'Those who enjoy basketball, step forward,' the trainer calls out.

Obulejo is among those who step into the circle. So is Mondua. The two exchange a smile.

'Look around you,' the trainer says. 'See who is in this group with you. Notice who also shares your love of basketball.'

Obulejo looks around. He sees some familiar faces, but one is a great surprise. The serious, sedate mathematics teacher, Mrs Hokkeina, is a basketball lover!

'Now step back to your original place in the circle.'

'In this activity you have given your attention to what you have in common with others,' the trainer says, 'not to your differences. You can see the things you share with others, and the many different groups you may belong to.'

On the way back to his shelter that day, Obulejo finds himself humming the *cwa* song, which he first heard as a tiny child. The familiar words spring to his lips.

'*Cwa iyo Eriani cwa*
Ka merek te Eriani
Ooh cwa iyo Eriani
Cwa ote mereke ca Eriani'

Lightheartedly he follows the song's rhythm once again, calls to the imaginary person, Eriani, to come quickly, because the weaver bird is eating her seeds. Mama Josephina sang that song as she went about her chores, and when Obulejo danced to it, Mama Josephina laughed and hugged her small son.

Obulejo remembers the great tree that grew close to his home in the mountains: there were dozens of *cwa* nests hanging from its spreading branches. He never succeeded in counting them all. He used to shin up that tree and call out to Riti and they would shout back and forth to each other and the weaver birds would fuss and flap and dive at them: how the friends laughed!

Obulejo is still humming as he enters the shelter. No one is home, and no meal has been prepared, but nothing can dampen Obulejo's spirits today.

He has discovered that he is connected in many ways to a whole lot more people than he had imagined. No need to fret because the household is changing. Ochan will always be his friend, and he will always be grateful to Maku and the others for the time they have spent together, whatever tensions may have arisen.

New possibilities are opening up. He is learning that it is possible to make peace, even in a refugee camp.

But best of all, Malia likes him; he is sure of it!

OBULEJO'S DAYS ARE almost too full, now, with daily chores, teaching his classes, attending mass on Sundays and peace education training after school three days a week on top of everything else. It's a struggle at times to fit it all in: the only thing he could possibly cut out is choir, but that would mean no music during the week and missing out on seeing Malia. She's always surrounded by her friends but most days he can get a few words with her, and when they sing together his heart soars. He really, really likes this girl.

He's excited when Father Angelo obtains permission for some of the young people in the choir to sing at a special service in Nairobi. It will be great to get away from Kakuma even for a few days, and he'll be with Malia for three whole days, albeit under the watchful eye of Father Angelo and the other chaperones. He is bitterly disappointed when he learns that Malia's uncle refuses to allow her to go on the trip. Perhaps her uncle has heard about her friendship with Obulejo and wants to make sure it goes no further. He must be careful. Malia's uncle is notoriously hot tempered. Obulejo does not want to get her in trouble. Or himself, either.

He must focus on his many other activities, and be patient. Hold his feelings for Malia in a secret corner of his heart.

As the peace course continues, the trainees are presented opportunities to make friends of former enemies, face difficult issues without resorting to violence, and join with others to work out solutions to problems as a group. Obulejo is always glad when Mondua is assigned to his group: it makes him feel he's just that little bit closer to Malia.

He has no trouble understanding and grasping the concepts presented by the trainers and often finds himself impatient with those who struggle with the ideas and practices. He is surprised how irritated he is made by the views of some of his fellow trainees.

He tries earnestly to listen carefully to them and speak calmly and courteously, but at times he finds it hard not to interrupt or challenge a fellow trainee, and sometimes he has to fight down the urge to slap that person hard! And when it's a senior man or woman, he feels guilt and shame at his impatience with them.

Like all Ma'di children, he has been drilled from earliest childhood in *laru* – respect – addressing all adults as auntie or uncle, deferring to the elders, accepting their views on all matters and following their instructions without hesitation or question.

But in his life as a refugee he's had to abandon some of those precepts, and learn to look out for himself even when it means trespassing on the rights of others or ignoring their needs. Besides, he realises, the ways of the elders have not necessarily created peace, but have sometimes kept the clans and tribes in conflict.

He feels ashamed of these new thoughts, but he cannot deny them.

This peace education is more complicated than it seemed.

One afternoon the trainer presents them with a new challenge.

'I'd like someone to give us an example of an actual conflict, one that is going on right now, where you live,' she says.

A schoolteacher, Mrs Gisemba, volunteers.

'The problem began in class,' Mrs Gisemba says. 'I did not see the incident, but I knew that two Acholi boys, Kidega and Olum, were involved.'

The Acholi speakers in the group waggle their heads when they hear these names, and one quickly translates for the rest of the group. Kidega in Acholi means 'not wanted, born of a mother hated by her husband's family', and Olum means 'born away from home', a name given to many of the children in the camp.

Mrs Gisemba continues. 'At first, neither boy would explain what had happened. But later Olum told me that Kidega had snatched his pencil and when Olum tried to get it back Kidega first of all denied he had taken it and then he slapped Olum and said he would beat him if Olum said anything. Kidega is much bigger than Olum and most of the smaller children are scared of him.'

Obulejo feels a rush of sympathy for the smaller boy.

Mrs Gisemba goes on. 'The next day I learned that Olum had gone home crying, without his pencil, and told his family what had happened, and his father immediately confronted Kidega's father, and defended his son. Kidega's father, to defend *his* son, called the other man a liar and demanded that the insult be withdrawn. Olum's father refused.

Other family members and clansmen got involved then and now real trouble is about to erupt.'

The other trainees nod. The scenario is only too familiar.

'The boys are from different clans and the two clans started insulting and threatening one another. "Step aside," the parents were told, "this is now a clan matter." Olum's clan demanded blood money for the slap Olum had suffered, but Kidega's clan refused. They reminded Olum's clan of the many attacks they had carried out on them; girls raped, kinsmen killed.'

'And the outcome?' the trainer asks.

'I think there will be widespread fighting, and very soon,' Mrs Gisemba says sadly.

The trainer turns to the rest of the group. 'What if you were the teacher in this situation?' she asks them. 'If Olum and Kidega were your pupils, what would you do to help solve this dispute? Where would you begin? Let's brainstorm some ideas.'

People call out suggestions and the trainer quickly compiles a list on the blackboard. Their next task is to discuss each suggestion and decide which ones might actually work.

'The idea is to draw on the life skills of the people involved,' the trainer reminds them.

But the calm exchange of ideas is derailed almost immediately when somebody mutters, 'Since the skills in this case are thieving and bullying, there is no peaceful solution possible. Can a leopard change its spots?'

An Acholi man responds angrily. 'Are you saying Acholi are liars and thieves?'

'No,' the other man replies, 'but the victim's father deserves an apology and the thief should be beaten for his sins. If this cannot happen, then Olum's family must fight Kidega's.'

Others join in the debate. Conflicting views are thrown back and forth.

'If we continue this way the violence will only get worse.'

'We will all be lost.'

'Pah, the child who stole should be punished.'

'The family must be avenged.'

'But isn't that what starts all wars?'

'It is up to the teachers to punish the child.'

'The parents are not the ones to blame!'

'What can parents do to protect their children?'

'We will all be victims if we don't protect our own.'

'It's this rotten war. Blame the government!'

People begin to shout. Obulejo feels like shouting, too, he's so angry. That stupid man who made those remarks about the Acholi, and those older men and women who said the boys should be beaten and the parents thrashed, they ought to have their heads banged together! What are they thinking? How can the children learn peaceful ways when adults are so intolerant?

And the trainer – why doesn't she do something? Is that all this peace education amounts to – playing games and charades, but when it comes to an actual conflict, let the same old violence prevail? Doesn't anyone but Obulejo understand what's at stake?

The long, long, hot session drags on. The group reaches no agreement. But what really sets Obulejo's blood boiling is the comment of a Dinka man: 'We must all share the responsibility for creating peace because we all created the war.'

Typical Dinka, Obulejo thinks. They start a war and then expect everyone else to share the blame.

'Speak for yourself,' Obulejo blurts out. 'It is you Dinkas who dragged us into this war. The Ma'di are a peaceful people. We don't wage war.'

'Oh no?' an Acholi man retorts.

Others grin. The never-ending skirmishes between the Ma'di and Acholi in times past are common knowledge.

'No, they leave it to the Dinka,' another chips in, 'then run away and hide behind the skirts of Mother Church.'

Eventually, the trainer winds up the discussion. She asks Mrs Gisemba to let the group know the outcome of the problem between the two students, and then dismisses everyone.

Obulejo leaves that session fuming, and deep into the night goes over and over the discussion, the things he said and what everybody else said. It's almost dawn before the penny drops. He's no different from anyone else, he realises; he's just as caught up in old hatreds and prejudices. Isn't he angry at Malia's uncle for keeping him from Malia, and wouldn't he like to force Uncle's hand? And when he tries to imagine a way the conflict between Mrs Gisemba's two Acholi families might be solved without blood being shed, he can't. The old conflicts are too deeply ingrained, the mistrust too long-standing.

As if in response to that thought, Obulejo catches the sound of running feet, and shouts begin to ring out. As the footsteps and shouting get closer Obulejo hunches low on his mat and edges away from the entrance. Maku is on watch outside, he knows, but one person alone is nothing against a gang intent on looting and killing. The footsteps pick up pace and the yelling and screaming intensifies until Obulejo expects the door to burst open and a rifle-wielding marauder to rush in. But no, the footsteps pass by and then retreat into the distance and the yells become fainter: some other unfortunate inmate is the target tonight.

The next day brings sobering but all too familiar news – a dozen men and boys kidnapped by the Rebels during the night, and three shelters in Obulejo's sector robbed and their occupants brutally beaten. One of the victims is not expected to survive. Obulejo doesn't catch his name. Rumours fly about. Women raped, a child slaughtered, someone chopped with a panga.

In the schoolyard and in the staffroom there is much talk of revenge. And is it just his imagination, Obulejo wonders, or are his pupils more unruly and troublesome than usual today? The boys pushing and scuffling and the girls pinching each other, fidgeting and fussing and name-calling. Everyone is unsettled. The daydreamers gaze about even more vacantly than usual, pupils Obulejo has taken great pains to help and encourage stumble more when reading aloud and even the most capable don't seem able to do the simplest sums.

As the day drags on, his patience starts to fray. And though he hates to admit it, he is unnerved by this latest outbreak of lawlessness. Are the attacks becoming more frequent? A dismal prospect. He reminds himself that at least there is choir practice to look forward to today, and relishes the prospect of joyful *adungu* music, dancing, singing and the chance to be near Malia.

But when he arrives in the square, neither Malia nor her sister Mondua is there.

'Have they been delayed?' Obulejo asks one of Malia's friends.

She does not answer.

'Are they ill?' he asks another.

The girls put their heads down and turn away, which makes Obulejo uneasy. Where are Malia and Mondua? They've never missed choir before. Something must have happened. Could they have been taken in last night's raid? Surely not; it's boys the Rebels want, not girls.

His mind races. Why won't the girls tell him where Malia is?

Suddenly it comes to him. Robbers. That must be it. Malia was attacked by those thieves he heard racing past in the night – Mondua too. Those jackals, how dare they! But they won't get away with it; he'll find them and punish them. He'll kill them! He'll go and find the girls' uncle straightaway, and tell him that he, Obulejo, will join the avengers.

Before he can act on his plan he is intercepted by Maku, who strides towards him.

'I must go,' Obulejo says, after briefly shaking Maku's proffered hand. 'I have urgent business to attend to.'

'More urgent than leading the singing?' Maku says. 'You and Malia are the only ones who can teach this song and she is not here today —'

'Yes yes,' Obulejo says bitterly, 'I know about her being attacked by robbers. Now please, I must go.'

'Not so fast,' Maku says. 'My friend, you are mistaken. Malia has not been attacked by anything, as far as I have been informed, except illness.'

Obulejo's heart skips a beat. 'She is ill?'

'Cholera, I'm afraid.'

The blood drains out of Obulejo's face. Cholera is far worse than being bashed by robbers. Everyone fears it. It spreads like wildfire, and there are few doctors in Kakuma and not enough antibiotics. Sick people die every day.

'Mondua too?' Obulejo says.

Maku nods his head. 'They are both very ill. We can only pray that they recover.'

Obulejo has seen how quickly cholera can turn a healthy person into a ravaged skeleton. But not Malia, surely – it cannot be possible. But he knows only too well that it can. The worst thing is that there is nothing he can do to help Malia. The hospital will not let him see the sisters, and even if they did he might carry the disease back and spread it to others.

His heart is not really in the singing that afternoon. He misses Malia's soprano accompanying his tenor. He misses her shy presence, and he is racked with worry for her. Getting sick is one of the most dangerous things that can happen to a person in a refugee camp.

Have Malia and Mondua been using the filthy water the Turkana trade with the inmates? he wonders. Their uncle should have seen to it that they had clean water. Everybody knows about the animal and human faeces in the water the Turkana peddle. Only the most desperate resort to using it.

Hah! There *is* something he can do to help, he realises: he can fetch clean water for the sisters, and use some of his precious shillings to buy them some soap. Clean water and soap are the two best defences against cholera – that is, if Malia and her sister are not already too ill.

When Obulejo finally arrives home close on dark that evening, he is completely exhausted. What a day! No sooner had his fears about the sisters being hurt by robbers proved false than the news of their illness crashed in on him, and instead of searching for wrongdoers and punishing them brutally he has walked miles and waited hours in line to fetch clean water and carry it to the hospital for them, then risked going to the market late in the day to purchase bars of soap as well.

And he will keep doing it, he vows, as long as they are ill.

25

WHEN HE JOINS the other trainees for the next peace education session, it takes Obulejo a few minutes to properly focus, so preoccupied is he with worry about Malia and her sister. The girls are no better, he has learned, but neither are they any worse – that is at least some cause for hope.

Finally he directs his attention to the front of the class. On the blackboard, chalked in wobbly capitals, are two lines of writing. Firstly a question:

IF I WISH TO CHANGE THE WORLD WHERE MUST I START?

And on the next line, the answer:

I MUST START WITH MYSELF.

Obulejo reads the sentences through, impatiently. *The 'if' in the first line is unnecessary*, he thinks. *Of course the trainees want to change the world, that's why they're here.* That's why he's prepared to work with both friends and enemies. And if he were in charge he would put an end to war, demand that everybody live in peace, and that people treat each other with kindness and respect.

He reads the two sentences again. The second one stops him in his tracks. *I MUST START WITH MYSELF.*

The words feel as if they are burning themselves into his brain. Accusing him. He looks around. Are the words having the same effect on other trainees? It seems not. People are chatting and laughing. A few are flipping through notebooks, or copying the sentences down.

He'd like to rub the words off the board and pretend he hasn't seen them. Surely he's doing his part by training children to co-operate with each other and find peaceful solutions, and by being tolerant of those in the training group? What more do they expect?

But then he thinks about the times he's used violence against others. He's always excused himself by saying that he has no choice. But is it really true, and is that how a peace-maker should act? The other day he was blaming colleagues for their ignorance and laying the responsibility for any conflict on the elders and leaders. Does he have any peaceful alternatives to offer? No.

The shadows lengthen and the heat of the day begins to fade. The sun is a red fireball behind the endless rows of camp barracks. At this time of day, back home, the family would be gathering wood, uncles carrying home logs and children dragging bundles of sticks for the evening fire. The mamas and sisters would be stirring the pots from which enticing aromas would float. Home. Comfort. Certainty. Family, one door, enclosing him protectively.

Obulejo's mind races back to a day in the gardens when he was a small child and the big rains came suddenly and flooded the creek. The children could not cross to get back to the village. The little ones were frightened. 'How will we get home?' they whimpered. And even while the bigger children were trying to reassure them, shouts reached them from the further bank, and there came the mothers and fathers, wading into the floodwaters to fetch their children and bear them safely home through the floods.

All that has been lost. *No one will come for me in Kakuma*, Obulejo thinks. *There is no one to take me safely back home.*

His musing is interrupted when the trainer enters and the classroom shuffles to order. It is an older man today. He picks up the pointer and raps it against the words on the board. The class reads the words aloud several times in unison. They are asked to consider the statement over the course of today's session and in the ensuing days.

Then the trainer tells them a story.

'There was an old man,' he begins, 'who had spent his life trying to change the world for the better. Long and hard he laboured until, in old age, he at last admitted defeat.

'"I have not changed the world," the old man told his family. "I have failed. It has been too big a task and I am just one man."

'So he decided he must be less ambitious. He would change his country. There was much that was unjust in the land of his birth and many who suffered. So he struggled and struggled to persuade the leaders to change their ways, but they refused to heed his calls.

'Defeated, the man turned to his local community. "All right," he said, "if I cannot change the world and I cannot change my country, then I will change my local community. I will persuade people who live in my district to care for one another and to stop quarrelling and fighting."

'A few people were persuaded, but largely the man's efforts came to nothing. Exasperated, the man turned his attention to his family. "As the head of my family," he declared, "if I cannot change things here, if I cannot bring peace, then I have achieved nothing. My life has been lived to no purpose."

'His wives smiled and the uncles scowled, and the aunts and sisters and brothers waited to see. The old man did his best, but you know families. When he met resistance even there the old man threw up his hands in despair. All his life he had striven to change things, to persuade people to act more kindly, and to create peace, and it had been for nothing. He might as well die. His life had been wasted.

'As he sat pondering these dismal thoughts, a tiny grandchild came toddling through the compound. Then she stumbled and fell. She held up her tiny grazed hands and began to wail. Irritated by the wailing, the old man looked around for the child's mother, or an elder grandson or daughter to tend to her. It was not his job to look after children.

'But as the child continued to weep, the old man began to look at things in a new way. The little girl was hurt. He had witnessed her tumble. She needed comforting. He was close by. It was that simple.

'He gathered her in his arms and patted away her tears, soothed her sore palms and carried her to a shady spot by the brush fence. And he was surprised to discover that although the burden on his arms had increased, the burden in his heart had lightened.'

There is a long silence at the end of the story.

When the trainer asks for feedback, the discussion is heated. Some argue that the old man employed the wrong methods. He should have gathered a group to make new laws and to enforce the peace. People should have listened to him. What sort of community disregards the advice of an elder? And the mother of the baby, or her older brothers and sisters, should have looked after the tot more conscientiously. Why had a tiny child been left to roam alone and allowed to come to harm?

A few remain silent. For Obulejo there is no need for discussion. The message in the story drops into his heart as clearly as any of the teaching stories Moini told his children by the fire at night.

'And what is the biggest change we all need to make, each and every one of us, in order to have peace?' the trainer asks.

A few suggestions are offered. The trainer writes them all on the board. Shifting opinions, overcoming prejudices, getting children to understand that co-operating, helping each other and finding solutions together are better than fighting.

'Yes, all good points,' the trainer says. 'And what is the concept that underlies these?'

Obulejo raises his hand.

The trainer nods.

'Changing our own attitudes.'

The trainer nods again. 'Good answer. In what way?'

'One door,' Obulejo replies.

Then, realising he has lapsed into Ma'di, he translates quickly. 'Family. Not clans and tribes and nations, but family. One family.'

He sits back down. A clamorous discussion breaks out around him, but he sees and hears none of it. He is busy pondering this revelation – this pathway to peace. Accepting everybody as part of his family.

Is it possible? Everybody one big family? Even the Dinka? Or is that a jump too high? In Dadaab it was the Somalis he had to watch out for, who visited harm on the Christian Sudanese, and they were frightening enough, but it is the Dinka who are really to blame for Obulejo's plight. He cannot forgive them, not while he's still in danger of their tribesmen kidnapping him and carting him off to fight.

He can co-operate with the Dinka trainees during games and exercises, but at what price can he truly think of them as brothers and sisters? By giving up his Ma'di ways? It's who he *is*, he can't change that. His thoughts and feelings and hopes and aspirations are those of a Ma'di. *And the prejudices*, a small inner voice whispers, but he discounts it. He is not to blame for how things are; the troubles started long before he was born!

But the story of the old man will not let him be. It is the Ma'di way to teach and learn through stories – and the meaning of this story is very clear. To help his granddaughter the old man had to step out of his traditional role and be willing to take on the work of younger people, of girls and women. It made no sense to leave the child weeping while he shouted for someone else to come and help her. He was the one on the spot. He had seen her fall and he was the best person to help her – because he was *there*.

As I am here, Obulejo admits, reluctantly. *Not because I want to be, or because I created the war, but because it's where life has brought me. And if I sit and wait for the leaders to bring peace, I am like the old man who waited his whole life before he understood what he needed to do. When I thought harm had come to Malia, my immediate desire was to punish others. And what would that have achieved but more violence? How can I be an educator for peace when what I really wanted was to fight and kill?*

As if in answer to Obulejo's unspoken question, the trainer invites Mrs Gisemba to come out the front and address the group.

'You all remember the story she told you?' he says. 'I too have been informed of it. And now today she will tell you the way it ended.' Obulejo drags his mind to attention.

'You will recall there was a problem with two of my students, Olum and Kidega,' Mrs Gisemba says. 'This problem quickly escalated to involve their families and clansmen. I became alarmed at how fast things were moving, and went to speak with one family and then the other, but they told me that it was no longer a school matter and it should be left to the clans to deal with. I knew that many people were going to get hurt, maybe even killed, and as I had no authority to talk with these clans, I went to some of my male colleagues and we decided it was time to test out what we have been learning.

'They went and spoke with the clan leaders,' she continues, 'and asked them to remember that the fighting at home was what they had fled from and that perpetuating the old quarrels would not help; there had to be another way. They were there for many hours; meanwhile I spoke to Kidega and Olum separately. Remember, Kidega had denied taking Olum's pencil. But now, alarmed at the trouble he had caused, he was willing to admit to the theft.

'"I did not want to give it back to Olum," he told me, "and I thought I could keep him from telling on me by slapping him – he is much smaller than me."

'"Are you brave enough to tell your parents this is what happened?" I asked him then, and he said yes.

'Kidega's parents were shocked when they heard the truth. So were the clans. They realised that a small incident between two boys was not something that should lead people to fight each other. Kidega's parents apologised for their son's actions and Olum's parents responded by saying they would not demand blood money. So the fight did not take place.'

Mrs Gisemba pauses. Obulejo glances from her to the trainer. The trainer's face is glowing.

'There is one final part to this story,' Mrs Gisemba adds. 'Soon afterwards I was walking home from school when I caught sight of Kidega's father.

'"Let's walk together," I said to him, "I am going to visit friends."

'We walked to the neighbouring sector and there coincidentally we came upon Olum's father, who bade us both come in and made us welcome, as traditional courtesy requires. We went in and were served food by the women and girls. Kidega's father seemed very uncomfortable to find himself the guest of a former enemy, but, bound by the rules of hospitality, he conducted himself with dignity and politeness and by the end of the meal conversation was flowing easily.

'When we rose to leave, Kidega's father invited Olum's father to come and have a meal with his family the following week.

'"I will gladly come," Olum's father replied, and the two men parted friends.'

Spontaneous applause greets Mrs Gisemba's account. She resumes her seat, a little flustered.

'Our colleague has presented us with an excellent example of the effective way peace education can work,' the trainer says.

Obulejo, like his fellow trainees, is silent as he ponders the story he has just heard.

26

OBULEJO WAITS ANXIOUSLY for news of Malia, and when Mondua at last returns to the group, a little shaky and a whole lot thinner, Obulejo approaches her shyly.

'Are you fully recovered?' he asks.

'I am, thank you,' Mondua replies. 'And my sister is getting better too. She is very weak, but gradually she is coming back to us.'

A great burden rolls off Obulejo's shoulders.

'Thanks to God!' he exclaims.

Mondua smiles. 'My uncle is aware of your service to us both and says he is in your debt.'

Obulejo blushes hotly and waves away the compliment.

'Malia is very precious to him,' Mondua continues. 'His own daughters were lost in the fighting and we are the only family he has left.'

No wonder her uncle guards the sisters so closely! Obulejo thinks.

'You may find that Uncle will have fewer objections to your friendship with my sister,' Mondua says. Then she smiles broadly. 'Within limits of course.'

'Of course.' Obulejo knows how a good Ma'di boy should behave. His blush deepens but his heart sings. Malia will recover! When he thinks what might have happened – no, it is too awful to imagine. He will treat her like a precious gem; he will take great care not to displease her family, and one day maybe . . .

But he must not think too far ahead. It is enough that Malia will soon be standing beside him in the choir. That she will sing and dance again. And that he is allowed to be her friend. Life has so many twists and turns. And in time they may be more than friends. That is his hope. But friendship is a good start.

The mamas will love Malia, he thinks. He imagines Malia in his family compound, Mama Josephina and Mama Natalina fussing over her, the aunties and uncles congratulating them both, and himself a proud and happy bridegroom. Such feasting and dancing there will be . . .

He pulls himself up abruptly. In spite of his resolve, he has raced far ahead into a future he can only dream about, for now. But he can tell his secret dream to his friends Ochan and Maku; they will rejoice with him.

And they do. Maku shakes his hand warmly and bids him proceed with care, but Ochan claps his friend on the shoulder and shouts aloud for joy.

Out in the dusty school compound under a glaring sun, Obulejo and the other peace education trainees are engaged in yet another exercise.

A group of them are instructed to join hands in a circle and tangle themselves into a knot, keeping their hands tightly linked the whole time. Soon the group becomes a laughing, sweaty mass, tightly coiled together. Everyone is pressed up against one another, arms over and under each other's. What now? they ask. The trainer introduces an outsider, and gives her the task of untangling the knot of people without breaking the links.

'This person was not present when the tangle was created,' the trainer says, 'and now it is her task to restore the circle to order.'

Obulejo watches closely as the outsider tries to work out where to start. Untangling the knot takes her several minutes of strenuous effort. When the circle is at last restored the group is instructed to get itself into a tangle a second time, but this time everyone is asked to take notice of the way they create the knot. In no time at all they become hopelessly twisted together once again.

'This time,' the trainer announces, after calling the helplessly laughing trainees to order, 'your task is to untangle yourselves on your own, without outside help.'

Everyone is amazed and delighted at how quickly and easily the task is accomplished the second time around, so much more simply and efficiently than when an outsider had tried to do it for them. It is the practical proof of what Obulejo had said in his interview: people hold the solution in their own hands and need to work together to find it. He looks forward to doing this exercise with his students.

Next comes the exclusion game. The trainees are reminded that it's just a game, and warned not to hold on to any feelings that come up, but to learn from these feelings and then let them go.

Obulejo and some of the other participants stand in a circle, hands linked, so that they form a tightly knit and unified group. One trainer then takes a smaller group aside, out of earshot of the main group.

Meanwhile a second trainer tells Obulejo's group, 'Your role is to refuse entry to anyone who asks to be let in to the group. Keep them on the outside. Do not allow them in. Keep your hands tightly linked and do not make a space for them. Don't let them become part of your circle.'

One after another the outsiders seek, by pleas and gestures, to be allowed to join the circle. Those in the circle refuse. Some of the outsiders plead piteously, others threaten. Some give up easily, accepting the refusal; others persist and try several times, pulling at the hands of those who will not let them in. The atmosphere changes. This is no longer a game.

A quiet young Somali woman, clad in veil and long gown, approaches the place in the circle where Obulejo is standing, hands linked with a fellow Ma'di on one side and a tall Dinka lad on the other. The Somali girl politely but strongly requests permission to be let in. Her eyes plead but her manner is dignified and contained. Obulejo finds it almost impossible to deny her, but his partners grip his hands more firmly and refuse to allow Obulejo to let the girl in. She moves on. Others refuse her entrance as well.

For a moment Obulejo is ashamed of his weakness, for being tempted to break the rules of the game and give in to the Somali girl, instead of standing strong. Then, he feels a mental shift, like the old man in the story who picked up the crying child.

Suddenly light-headed, he wonders if he is going to faint. Then the fog clears and he knows what he must do.

The braveness he has sought all his life is not to be found in fighting wars or facing baboons or in intimidating others. It is something stronger, less visible, deeply private.

This time, when the Somali girl approaches, Obulejo tugs his hand loose from his partner's and holds it out to the girl. She takes it, flashing thanks with her eyes, and he quickly draws her into the circle. He nods to his partner to take the girl's other hand. The rangy young Dinka is unwilling. He scowls at Obulejo. Obulejo looks back steadily.

'It was your countryman who saved my life,' he says quietly. 'You are my brother.'

The Somali girl's eyes are brimming with unshed tears.

'Our sister,' Obulejo mouths to the Dinka lad and nods to the girl.

The exchange takes only a few seconds, but to Obulejo it seems that an eternity passes before a broad grin breaks over his partner's face and he snatches up the girl's other hand. They have not followed the rules of the exercise, but this way everyone wins. No one need be left out. Together Obulejo and his Dinka partner closed the gap.

The circle is once again unbroken.

EPILOGUE

OBULEJO WAKES WITH a start, rubs his eyes and gazes about him. He cannot make sense of where he is. Everything is unfamiliar.

Through the window comes the braying sound of vehicles and a cacophony of voices chattering in Swahili. The air is thick with the scent of diesel and crumbling concrete.

The old feeling of dread begins to clutch Obulejo's stomach. What has happened? Where is he?

He springs out of bed, ready to flee.

Then he remembers. This is not Kakuma. It's Nairobi. He's in the holding centre, with his wife and baby son, waiting for a flight. It's his last day in Africa. His last day as a refugee. Tomorrow they will begin the journey to Australia and a new life. It hardly seems real. And yet the maroon folder on the floor beside the striped carry bag of belongings for the journey shows that it is. The folder contains their exit visas and travel documents.

For another journey into the unknown, but this time with a happier outcome.

A new home in a new country with no war.

Obulejo glances back to where his young wife lies, still sleeping, oblivious to her husband's wakefulness, her arm curled protectively around their young son. The last few weeks have been exhausting for her. Since their application to migrate to Australia was approved there has been a flurry of last-minute medicals, endless paperwork and frantic preparations for the journey ahead. Obulejo is anxious to get underway, but also feels torn about leaving Africa and giving up any possibility of ever finding his parents and brothers and sisters. Malia will be his family now, and his little boy, Ambayo.

Obulejo thinks back to when he met Malia, five years ago. It had been hard to break down Uncle's resolve to protect his niece from the advances of young men, but little by little Obulejo had accomplished it, by always showing great respect to Uncle, not singling Malia out for special attention and not pressing his suit too forcefully. What had probably convinced Uncle that Obulejo could take good care of his niece was that a few months after completing the peace education training, Obulejo was chosen to become a trainer of peace educators, a position as a UNHCR employee that carried a great deal of respect, and also a regular salary. Finally, after much negotiation, a bride price had been agreed upon – a percentage of Obulejo's salary – and the nuptials were completed.

Obulejo had then broached the subject of applying for resettlement overseas. Uncle was in favour. They would all travel together.

'Should you and Malia be blessed with children,' Uncle said, 'it is best that they grow up far from war.'

Obulejo had applied three times and three times his application had failed. Then Ambayo arrived, whose name meant 'growing up without elders', a sorrowful fate for a Sudanese child, but God willing the child would grow up in a peaceful land, far away from Sudan's troubles, and Obulejo redoubled his efforts till at last he was rewarded with success. He and Malia and Ambayo, along with Malia's uncle and sister, were accepted by Australia for resettlement in Tasmania.

The first thing Obulejo notices when he steps off the plane in Hobart is the taste and texture of the air. Cold and salty, it prickles his nose hairs and makes his eyes water. So different from South Sudan. The sky is lower, too, a duller blue than at home, and the light is different. Everything is different. *As am I*, he thinks with a mixture of excitement and dismay, a married man and a father, arriving in a new country in new warm clothes and brand-new boots which will carry him and his small family into a different future. Even his name is different. Printed in his passport is his new name, Joseph Moini. Joseph, the name the missionaries had given him at his baptism, meaning 'he will add' – then his father's name – Moini. That's one of the new things he's learned, that in Australia you need two names, your own and your father's. He rolls the new name on his tongue. Its taste is so different from 'Obulejo'. Perhaps no one will ever call him Obulejo again, now his family are lost to him.

I must not think about my family, he tells himself sternly. *I must not think about home. I must think only about my new life in a new country.* He takes Malia's arm, and they start across the windy tarmac to the terminal.

If only it were not so cold, Obulejo thinks, as a spiteful breeze caresses his close-cropped head, the wind's icy fingers brushing his chilled nose and aching ears. He wraps his son more closely in his jacket and presses onwards.

A sea of white faces greets the new arrivals. Then Obulejo spots a cluster of black ones, towards the rear of the crowd. A hand waves. Obulejo waves back. White faces surround them and everywhere is the barely intelligible jabber of English; nowhere the familiar sound of Arabic, Ma'di or Swahili. The Sudanese arrivals peer out of startled eyes. White people stare back, covertly, wondering who these shivering, bewildered-looking people are. The Sudanese travellers are tired, chilled and anxious, but they smile resolutely and shuffle forward.

A few of the older people hesitate. Their faces are stricken. They're grieving for home, for the dead they've left unburied, for children scattered across countries and continents, family that no longer exists. They're not ready for a new life; they want the familiar one back, but without the danger, even though they know the old life is gone as surely as unguarded gardens are stripped bare by baboons and the raiding weaver birds. They carry their grief quietly and with dignity, ready to make the best of things in this new country, although their sorrowful demeanour suggests their expectations are stained with doubt.

Most of the local Sudanese community is here to meet the new arrivals. They now press forward with extended hands. Greetings are exchanged and people hover and wait for their baggage. Children are fretful and tired and the mothers' faces are strained and anxious. Obulejo too is anxious. He will need to find a way to support his family and quickly. But hasn't he faced much harder challenges than this and overcome them? Everything will be all right: he knows it will. And who knows, maybe one day he will be reunited with those he has left behind.

Glancing at the apprehensive faces around him, Obulejo feels a stab of guilt for the burst of joy that suddenly explodes inside him. What is it in the air that is making his chest ache and his head reel? Not the cold, not the smell of the nearby salty ocean, not the long flight and the plummeting to earth – it is the scent of freedom. He inhales it with zest.

THE HISTORY OF THE SUDANESE CIVIL WAR

THE EXTENSIVE region once referred to as the Sudan extends some five thousand kilometres in a band several hundred kilometres wide across north-east and central Africa. Its name derives from the Arabic *bilād as-sūdān* (بلاد السودان), or 'land of the black peoples'.

Invasion, colonisation, slave trading and war are all part of the tumultuous history of Sudan.

When the British governed Sudan as a colony they administered the northern and southern provinces separately. The population of southern Sudan is primarily Christian and animist and considers itself culturally sub-Saharan, while most of the north is inhabited by Muslims who are culturally Arabic.

The south was therefore held to be similar to the other East African colonies – Kenya, Tanganyika (now Tanzania) and Uganda – while northern Sudan was more akin to Arabic-speaking Egypt.

In 1946, the British gave in to northern pressure to integrate the two areas. This integration took place without consultation with southern leaders. Arabic was made the language of administration in the south, and northerners began to hold positions there. The southern elite, trained in English, resented being kept out of their own government, and feared being subsumed by the political power of the larger north.

DECOLONISATION

After the February 1953 agreement by the United Kingdom and Egypt to grant independence to Sudan, internal tensions between the north and south heightened. Most of the power was given to the northern Muslim elites based in Khartoum, causing unrest in the south. Northern leaders seemed to be backing away from commitments to create a federal government that would give the south substantial autonomy. The south demanded representation and more regional autonomy. When this did not eventuate, civil war broke out in 1955.

THE FIRST SUDANESE CIVIL WAR (1955–1972)

Initially the war was waged largely by guerrilla forces, which were soon subsumed into a larger, more formidable fighting force, the southern Sudanese separatist army. This army became known as Anyanya, a term in the Ma'di language that means 'snake venom'. The first civil war thus became known as the Anyanya Rebellion or Anyanya. People in the south had suffered great injustice under the central government and wished to break free of it and experience greater self-determination. This was the cause behind which Anyanya rallied. But although the common goal was to gain autonomy for the south, conflict between the leaders of the rebellion and the eruption of old tribal rivalries and enmities often prevented effective and unified action by the rebel forces. And because of the collateral damage and intense suffering caused by the rebel armies, they were not always viewed positively by South Sudanese people. Half a million people died during the seventeen years of war and thousands more were forced to leave their homes.

ADDIS ABABA AGREEMENT

Mediation between the World Council of Churches (WCC) and the All Africa Conference of Churches (AACC) eventually led to the Addis Ababa Agreement of February 1972, bringing the conflict to an end. In exchange for ending their armed uprising, southerners were granted a single southern administrative region with various defined powers.

But the Addis Ababa Agreement proved to be only a temporary respite. The first violations of the agreement occurred when President Gaafar Nimeiry attempted to take control of oil fields straddling the north–south border. Uneven distribution of resources was a source of ongoing tension. Access to the oil fields meant significant economic benefit to whoever controlled them. The south was agriculturally richer as well, with higher rainfall than the north and an abundance of fertile land.

Islamic fundamentalists in the north were also discontented with the Addis Ababa Agreement, which gave relative autonomy to the non-Islamic majority in the south. The fundamentalists continued to grow in power, and in 1983 President Nimeiry declared all Sudan an Islamic state under sharia law, terminating the existence of the Southern Sudan Autonomous Region. War erupted once more.

THE SECOND SUDANESE CIVIL WAR (1983–2005)

The Sudan People's Liberation Army (SPLA) was founded in 1983 as a rebel group, to fight against the central government and to re-establish an autonomous southern Sudan. While based in southern Sudan, it identified itself as a movement for all oppressed Sudanese citizens, and was led by John Garang de Mabior. Initially, the SPLA campaigned for a 'United Sudan', criticising the central government for policies that were leading to national 'disintegration'. Traditional and long-standing tribal enmities and internal dissensions bedevilled the struggle, as they had during the first civil war and continue to do so, to this day.

By 2005, when a comprehensive peace agreement was signed in Nairobi, the Second Sudanese Civil War had become one of the longest on record. Four million people in southern Sudan were displaced at least once (and often repeatedly) during the war. Thousands ended up in refugee camps in Kenya and Uganda, many of these later relocating to Australia, Canada and the USA as humanitarian entrants.

Roughly two million people died as a result of violence, famine and disease caused by the conflict, one of the highest civilian death tolls of any war since World War II. The war was also marked by a large number of human rights violations, including slavery and mass killings, and armies from all sides enlisted children in their ranks.

COMPREHENSIVE PEACE AGREEMENT

The 2005 peace agreement required that child soldiers be demobilised and sent home, and guaranteed autonomy for the south for six years, to be followed by a referendum on independence in 2011. Oil revenues were to be divided equally between the government and SPLA during the six-year autonomy period, and Islamic sharia law was applied in the north, while terms of use of sharia in the south were to be decided by a more equally representative elected assembly.

REPUBLIC OF SOUTH SUDAN

In January 2011, a referendum was held to determine whether South Sudan should become an independent country and separate from Sudan. An overwhelming majority – 98.83 per cent – of the population voted for independence. Those living in the north and expatriates living overseas also voted.

The Republic of South Sudan formally became independent from Sudan on 9 July 2011, and is a Christian country. English has replaced Arabic as the official language of education and administration.

Disputes still remain, including over the division of oil revenues – 75 per cent of all the former Sudan's oil reserves are in South Sudan, and the oil-rich region of Abyei remains a disputed territory. Ongoing tribal conflicts and enmities continue to acerbate tensions and a very uneasy peace currently exists in both Sudan and the Republic of South Sudan.

AUTHORS' NOTES

AFTER MEETING in Hobart in 2011, Terry and Sarafino quickly decided to write Sarafino's life history, *A Little Peace*, together. The title of the book reflects the turbulent events of Sarafino's life: he was born in a refugee camp in Uganda, where his family had fled during the first phase of the Sudanese Civil War, and his schooldays were later interrupted when war broke out again and he was forced to trek through thick jungle to seek refuge in neighbouring Kenya. He spent more than ten years in refugee camps, training as a peace education facilitator in Kakuma before migrating to Tasmania in 2004.

While *A Little Peace* was still in production, Terry and Sarafino began to collaborate with other Tasmanian writers and artists and with Ma'di elder Paskalina Eiyo to create two bilingual picture books, *When I Was a Girl in Sudan* and *When I Was a Boy in Sudan*. These books are based on Sarafino's and Paskalina's childhood memories of daily life in Sudan before the war. They provide Ma'di and Australian children with a view of traditional Sudanese life and a taste of Ma'di language.

In 2012 Terry and Sarafino travelled to South Sudan together on a research trip. The trip awoke traumatic memories for Sarafino, but also joy, as he was reunited with members of his family he had not seen for twenty years. Terry witnessed first-hand the devastation many years of civil war had inflicted on the country, and both Terry and Sarafino wished to assist school students. They promised to send books when they returned to Australia.

A Little Peace, When I Was a Girl in Sudan and *When I Was a Boy in Sudan* were published in 2014. Book sales and a crowd-funding campaign will enable Terry and Sarafino to return to South Sudan, taking 2000 copies of the picture books for students in South Sudanese schools, and also copies of *A Little Peace* and *Trouble Tomorrow*, and many other books donated by Tasmanians.

ACKNOWLEDGEMENTS

WE SALUTE THE Ma'di people of South Sudan for their courage and resilience through decades of war. We hope that those who now have made Australia their home may find peace and freedom here.

We owe a great debt of gratitude to our families in Australia and South Sudan, in particular to Albino Okano who generously assisted every aspect of this book's creation and who continues to offer support and assistance both to us in Australia and to family and colleagues in South Sudan. We thank our respective partners, Beatrice Storrs and David Collins, for their support and the sacrifices they have made during the long years of research and writing.

Terry particularly thanks Tasmanian writer Julie Hunt for good conversation, enthusiasm and vital encouragement during those times Terry felt she might never see the book completed! Julie also introduced us to the team at Allen & Unwin, with whom we have developed a cordial relationship.

Thanks to commissioning editor Sarah Brenan for believing in the book, for her thoughtful editing, searching questions and excellent suggestions for strengthening the narrative; thanks to Sonja Heijn for her impressive and rigorous attention to all the little foxes that might potentially spoil the vine; to the sensitive and flexible cover designer and especially to Sophie Splatt who has midwifed *Trouble Tomorrow* through to its birth. It is our work for peace in the world and we thank all those, named and unnamed, who have helped bring it to completion.

ABOUT THE AUTHORS

DR TERRY WHITEBEACH is a Tasmanian writer and historian and the mother of two adult sons and two daughters. She has published in a number of genres including poetry, novels, radio drama and biography. *Trouble Tomorrow* is her third novel for teenagers.

SARAFINO ENADIO is a Ma'di man from South Sudan, who spent many years during the Sudanese Civil War in refugee camps in Kenya, before migrating to Tasmania. He works in education, and is currently studying for his Masters of Teaching.